# The CODE BUSTERS Club

CASE #5

The Hunt for the
Missing Spy

Penny Warner

MINNEAPOLIS

*To Yuka Hayashi, the inspiration for the*
*new Code Buster, Mika —Penny*

Darby Creek
A division of Lerner Publishing Group, Inc.
241 First Avenue North
Minneapolis, MN 55401 USA

For reading levels and more information, look up this title at www.lernerbooks.com.

Cover art by Victor Rivas.
Interior illustrations © Laura Westlund/Independent Picture Service.

Main body text set in Gazette LH Roman 12/21. Typeface provided by Adobe Systems.

**Library of Congress Cataloging-in-Publication Data**

Warner, Penny.
    The hunt for the missing spy / by Penny Warner.
        pages cm. — (Code Busters Club ; #5)
        Summary: During a class trip to Washington, D.C., the Code Busters have many opportunities to hone their sleuthing skills as they explore the International Spy Museum, the White House, and more, but when a classmate goes missing, a mysterious figure in a trench coat may be the key to solving the case.
        ISBN 978-1-5124-0304-6 (th : alk. paper) — ISBN 978-1-5124-0305-3 (EB pdf)
        [1. Cryptography—Fiction. 2. Ciphers—Fiction. 3. Missing children—Fiction. 4. Spies—Fiction. 5. Washington (D.C.)—Fiction. 6. Mystery and dectective stories.]
    I. Title.
PZ7.W2458Hun 2016
[Fic]—dc23                                                    2015017911S

Manufactured in the United States of America
1 – SB – 12/31/15

# CODE BUSTERS CLUB RULES

## Motto
To solve puzzles, codes, and mysteries and
keep the Code Busters Club secret!

## Secret Sign
Interlocking index fingers
(American Sign Language sign for "friend")

## Secret Password
Day of the week, said backward

## Secret Meeting Place
Code Busters Club Clubhouse

# Code Busters Club Dossiers

## IDENTITY: Quinn Kee

**Code Name:** "Lock&Key"

Description
Hair: Black, spiky
Eyes: Brown
Other: Sunglasses

**Special Skill:** Video games, Computers, Guitar

**Message Center:** Doghouse

**Career Plan:** CIA cryptographer
or Game designer

**Code Specialties:** Military code,
Computer codes

## IDENTITY: MariaElena—M.E.—Esperanto

**Code Name:** "Em-me"

**Description**
Hair: Long, brown
Eyes: Brown
Other: Fab clothes

**Special Skill:** Handwriting analysis, Fashionista

**Message Center:** Flower box

**Career Plan:** FBI handwriting analyst or Veterinarian

**Code Specialties:** Spanish, I.M., Text messaging

## IDENTITY: Luke LaVeau

**Code Name:** "Kuel-Dude"

**Description**
Hair: Black, curly
Eyes: Dark brown
Other: Saints cap

**Special Skill:** Extreme sports, Skateboard, Crosswords

**Message Center:** Under step

**Career Plan:** Pro skater, Stuntman, Race car driver

**Code Specialties:** Word puzzles, Skater slang

## IDENTITY: Dakota—Cody—Jones

**Code Name:** "CodeRed"

**Description**
Hair: Red, curly
Eyes: Green
Other: Freckles

**Special Skill:** Languages, Reading faces and body language

**Message Center:** Tree knothole

**Career Plan:** Interpreter for UN or deaf people

**Code Specialties:** Sign language, Braille, Morse code, Police codes

# CONTENTS

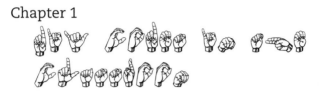

*To crack the chapter title code, check out the CODE BUSTERS' Key Book & Solutions on page 148, 157.*

# READER

*To see keys and solutions to the
puzzles inside, go to the Code Busters'
Key Book & Solutions on page 148.*

*To see complete Code Busters Club
Rules and Dossiers, and solve
more puzzles and mysteries, go to*
**www.CodeBustersClub.com**

# Chapter 1

"**D**oes anyone know what this code is?" Ms. Stadelhofer asked her sixth-grade students. She had just written ten unfamiliar curious symbols on the board.

Cody (Dakota) Jones, a member of the Code Busters Club, frowned at the characters. She guessed they were some kind of language, maybe Chinese or Japanese, but she didn't know which one.

Mika Takeda, the quiet new girl who sat across from Cody, slowly raised her hand. Cody was

1

surprised. This was the first time Mika had volunteered an answer since she arrived last week.

"It's Japanese," Mika said.

"Correct," Ms. Stad said, smiling warmly at the girl with short black hair. When Mrs. Stad had introduced Mika to the class, she had explained that the girl had recently come from Japan. But Mika hadn't said much in class and Cody didn't know much more about her. Cody remembered how shy she had felt when she was the new student at Berkeley Cooperative Middle School, and she planned to invite Mika to join her and her Code Busters Club members at lunch. It would be cool to get to know someone from another country.

"Do you know Japanese, Mika?" Cody asked.

The girl nodded. "Of course. I spoke it when I lived in Japan."

Ryan raised his hand, and Ms. Stad called on him.

"Chinese and Japanese kind of look the same."

"To people unfamiliar with the languages, they might, Ryan," Ms. Stad said. "The characters used are similar. But the vocabulary is different, and the grammar is different."

To Cody's surprise, Mika raised her hand again. "My Japanese books are different, too. They open from the back and are written in columns from top to bottom and right to left."

Interesting, Cody thought. She'd never seen a book written in Japanese.

"Mika speaks Japanese and English. How many of you can speak a language besides English?" Ms. Stad asked.

Half the class raised their hands. Cody's teacher asked which languages the students knew. M.E. said Spanish. Samir said his family spoke Hindi at home. Cole was learning Irish Gaelic from his grandfather. Jodie knew some Vietnamese, and Josh was studying Hebrew.

"Wow, I'm impressed at how multilingual you all are," Ms. Stad said.

Matt the Brat raised his hand. "I can speak Pig Latin. Is-say it-tay ime-tay or-fay ecess-ray?"

*Code Busters' Solution found on p. 153.*

The class laughed. Cody rolled her eyes. Ms. Stad looked at him sternly.

When the students finally quieted down, she announced, "Today I'm going to teach you a new code."

The class murmured their excitement.

Cody loved discovering new codes. That's why she and her friends, M.E. (MariaElena) Esperanto, Quinn Kee, and Luke LaVeau were in the Code Busters Club. Quinn had started the club by posting a sign in code, asking interested kids to contact him. Luke joined first, then M.E. and finally Cody. Together they had learned Morse code, Semaphore, Braille, hieroglyphs, and a bunch of other codes. They were also learning some different languages.

Cody had shown her friends American Sign Language (ASL), which she used with her deaf younger sister, Tana. M.E. had taught the group a few words in Spanish. Cody could already count to twenty, and say ¡hola! (hello), ¡adiós! (goodbye), and ¿Dónde está el baño? (Where's the bathroom?). Quinn was showing them how to write Chinese characters, such as 你好, ni hao, which meant "hello." And Luke had shared some words in Cajun French he'd learned while living in New Orleans, like *bonjour* ("bone-jur") for "hello," *c'est bon* ("say bone") for "that's good," and *gris-gris* ("gree-gree") for a "magic charm."

"I'm going to teach you some Japanese," Ms. Stad said.

"That's not code," Matt the Brat blurted out without raising his hand.

"Actually, it is," Ms. Stad said. "All languages are codes, including English. The letters stand for sounds and the words stand for concepts. It's just not a *secret* code if you know the language."

Cool, Cody thought. She could add Japanese to her list of languages she'd be learning.

"Why do we have to learn Japanese?" Matt the Brat whined. "I already have enough trouble speaking American. Besides, we're going to Washington, D.C. next week, not Japan."

Matthew Jeffreys was always complaining about something. Cody had learned to tune him out---most of the time, anyway. Unfortunately, he was a big guy—almost as tall as the teacher—and he sat right in front of Cody, so he wasn't that easy to ignore.

5

Ms. Stad sighed. "Because, Matthew, it will be cherry blossom time in the nation's capital when we arrive. The cherry blossom Festival is an important event that's been going on since the first cherry trees were brought from Japan in 1912—over a hundred years ago."

"What's so great about a bunch of trees?" Matt argued.

"The trees were a gift from the mayor of Tokyo, Japan, to the United States," Ms. Stad said, "to celebrate friendship between the two countries. Every year, we exchanges gifts with Japan. They shared their cherry trees with us, and we've shared our dogwood trees with them. And since we'll be in Washington, D.C. at cherry blossom time, we'll get to enjoy the festival."

"But I don't want to go to a *tree* festival!" Matt complained. "I just want to see the Spy Museum!"

"That's enough, Matthew," Ms. Stad said, crossing her arms in front of her. If you don't want to come on the trip, you can stay home, and I'll leave you plenty of homework to do. It's up to you."

Matt slumped down in his seat. *That should keep him quiet for a few minutes*, Cody thought. She was really looking forward to the spring trip to D.C. The sixth graders had worked hard to earn enough money for the trip. First, the Code Busters had gotten reward money for helping with a theft at the Rosicrucian Egyptian Museum. To get the rest of the money they needed, the sixth graders had done odd jobs like dog-walking and bake sales and car washes. While Cody was looking forward to seeing the Smithsonian museums, the presidential monuments, and the White House, she was pretty sure that the International Spy Museum would be the most exciting part of the trip.

She'd been checking the Spy Museum website every day for the past week, looking for information about the code-busting displays, notorious spies and their gadgets, and the cool stuff they could buy at the Spy Store. She wanted to get some supplies for the Code Busters Club, including a real decoder ring, a Caesar's Cipher wheel, and some invisible ink pens.

"Yes, class—and Matthew—the Spy Museum will be a fun part of the trip," Ms. Stad continued. "But back to our lesson. As you know, spies often communicated in code. And if you know a language that other people around you don't know, you can use it as a code. And knowing some Japanese will come in handy while we're in Washington, D.C. You'll see many signs in Japanese when we visit the Cherry Blossom Festival. That's why I'm going to teach you some Japanese characters."

"Cool," a couple of students said.

"Now, for homework . . ." Ms. Stad began.

Several students groaned.

"Your assignment will be to use these Japanese characters to crack a coded message." She pointed to the markings on the board.

Matt grumbled under his breath. Cody couldn't make out his words—not that she wanted to. She was excited to learn a new code and language. She and the other Code Busters Club members would definitely use it to send secret messages to each other.

"There's no direct translation for the English alphabet," Ms. Stad said, addressing the class, "but these are the numbers in Japanese from zero to nine."

| 〇 | 一 | 二 | 三 | 四 | 五 | 六 | 七 | 八 | 九 |
|---|---|---|---|---|---|---|---|---|---|
| 0 | 1 | 2 | 3 | 4 | 5 | 6 | 7 | 8 | 9 |

Ms. Stad pronounced each word as she pointed to it and the students repeated after her. "*Zero, ichi, ni, san, yon, go, roku, nana, hachi,* and *kyuu.*"

Cody carefully copied down the information from the board, trying to memorize the numbers as she went along. The zero was just a circle, just like in English. Easy-peasy. The number one was a dash—another easy one. The number 2 was made up of two dashes, the bottom one a little longer than the top one. And the number 3 was three dashes. So far they made sense.

The number 4 was a little harder. It looked like a square window made up of four lines, with curtains on either side. Relating the character to something would help her remember.

She counted the lines for the number 5—five!—

then memorized how they were put together—a lower case *h* inside a capital I, like "hI!"

Six looked like a person—head, arms, and two legs. Seven looked like a combination of *L* and *t*. Eight was easy—just two legs. And nine looked like a lower-case *t* and a backward capital *J* together.

The Japanese numbers wouldn't be too hard to memorize. And once she and the Code Busters learned them, they could write down meeting times and other numbers, and keep the information secret from snoops like Matt the Brat. She doubted Matt would bother to learn the lesson, so their messages would be safe from his prying eyes.

"Now," Ms. Stad said. "Can anyone of you figure out what this means?"

She drew four numbers in Japanese on the board.

一　八　五　五

Gabriella raised her hand. "One-eight-five-five."

Ms. Stad nodded. "Those are the right numbers, but what do you think they represent?"

M.E.'s hand shot up. "The year 1855?"

"Very good! Now what was significant about that year?"

A few hands went up but no one got the right answer. Finally Ms. Stad said, "That's the year the first Smithsonian Museum opened. I'll teach you some new words in Japanese every day until we leave for Washington, D.C.," Ms. Stad announced. "We'll also be learning some acronyms. An acronym is usually formed using the first letters of several words, such as ASAP, which stands for "as soon as possible", or BFF, which is "best friends forever." Today we'll start with the acronym FBI Does anyone know what FBI stands for? I'll give you a hint: its headquarters is located in Washington, D.C."

Cody raised her hand. This was an easy one for her. "Federal Bureau of Investigation."

"That's right," Ms. Stad said, "but there's also another meaning. Here's a list of acronyms you can figure out for extra credit homework."

Ms. Stad passed out a sheet of paper filled with capital letters. Cody looked it over and recognized most of them from texting.

| APB | DIY | OMW |
|-----|-----|-----|
| AWOL | EMT | PBJ |
| BLT | FAQ | P.I. |
| BOLO | FYI | S&R |
| BRB | LOL | UFO |

The bell rang, dismissing the class for the day. "Have a great afternoon, everyone!" Ms. Stad called out as the students began gathering their papers and backpacks. "Remember! Your homework is due tomorrow."

Cody and M.E. grabbed their backpacks and headed for the flagpole to meet the other Code Busters, Quinn and Luke. The boys were also in the sixth grade but in a different class. They had Mr. Pike.

"Six more days!" Cody announced as she and M.E. caught up with their friends. "I can't wait!"

"Me either," Quinn said. "I want to see the Washington Monument while we're there. Mr. Pike told us how George Washington used to write coded messages to his soldiers during the Revolutionary War. He gave us a copy of Washington's code. We're supposed to decipher a message for homework."

"Cool," M.E. said. "We learned how to write numbers in Japanese, and we're going to learn some acronyms, like FBI Let's write some codes for each other to solve when we get to the clubhouse."

As the Code Busters started walking in the direction of the Eucalyptus Forest, where their clubhouse was located, Quinn pulled out something dangling from Cody's backpack. "You almost lost your homework," he said, handing the paper to her. "It was about to fall out."

Cody frowned. She glanced at it, then shook her head. "This isn't my homework." She studied the cartoon drawings on the paper, wondering who had put the paper in her backpack.

After glancing at the artwork, she held up the paper for the others to see. "That's weird. It's just a bunch of random drawings."

"Maybe it's a coded message," Luke offered. "Like one of those rebus puzzles."

"What's it supposed to mean?" M.E. asked.

"I'm not sure," Cody answered.

"Let me see," Quinn said. He took the paper and studied it. "I think Luke's right. It looks like some kind of rebus code, where the pictures are supposed to represent words. The first one looks like the Eye of Horus. We learned about that when we went to the Rosicrucian Egyptian Museum."

"Why would someone draw the Eye of Horus?" Luke asked. "We're done studying ancient Egypt."

Quinn shrugged. "The next one is a clock."

"Yes, a clock," Cody said, then added, "or maybe a watch."

"Sure," Quinn agreed. "And then there's a sheep. So, we have the Eye of Horus, plus a watch, plus a sheep. And then a welcome sign. But I have no idea what it all means."

Cody took back the paper. "Okay, the Eye of Horus could just mean *eye*." She pointed to her eye.

"Or *I*," added M.E., pointing to herself.

Quinn nodded. "And the watch could mean *time*."

"Or *watch*," Cody said, pointing two fingers out from his eyes, the ASL sign for "watch."

"Okay, we've got 'I watch . . . ,'" Quinn said, "but what does *sheep* mean?"

"Maybe it's a *ewe*," M.E. said. "A female sheep."

Cody's eyes lit up. "Or *ewe* for the word *you*! That means it reads, 'I watch you.'"

"Like 'I'm *watching* you,'" Luke said.

"What does the last picture mean?" Luke asked.

"'Welcome'?" M.E. said. She shrugged. "That makes no sense."

"Well, at least we figured out most of it," Quinn said. "Let's work on the rest when we get to the clubhouse."

Cody read over the message once more before folding it up and putting it in her backpack. Why had someone put that note in her backpack? Was someone trying to scare her? Spy on her? But why? And who could it be?

She only had one clue to go on—whoever drew those pictures was a good artist.

And whoever it was had gotten close enough to her to stuff that paper in her backpack without her noticing.

Too close.

# Chapter 2

The gang soon arrived at their homemade structure hidden among the Eucalyptus trees. After their original secret meeting place had burned down, they'd rebuilt it in the same spot. They'd nailed the walls together using old billboard panels, sealed the corners with duct tape, and covered the top with a camouflage parachute they'd bought at the Army-Navy Surplus Store.

The makeshift door was padlocked on the outside and only the Code Busters had keys. But if one of the members got to the clubhouse first, he or she could unlock the door and then bolt it from the inside. When the others arrived, they'd have to give the secret knock—their initials in Morse code—and the password—the day of the week said backward, like "yadseut." There had been a couple of times when intruders had tried to break in, so the locks and bolts and knocks and passwords were definitely necessary.

After the kids removed their backpacks and settled onto the carpet-covered metal floor, they took out their homework assignments. The girls shared their newly learned Japanese numbers with the boys, who copied them into their secret Code Busters notebooks. Then the boys let Cody and M.E. copy the Washington code Mr. Pike had given them.

When they were finished, Quinn pulled out his mini tablet from his backpack and said, "I want to show you guys some cool stuff I found on the Spy Museum webpage." He typed in the words "International Spy Museum." When the home page came up, he showed it to the others. "There are hundreds of spy gadgets to check out when we get there. And you even become a spy when you enter the museum."

"I know!" Cody said, her face brightening. "I've been reading all about the place."

M.E. frowned. "You mean you get to be a real spy?"

Quinn shook his head. "No, it's just a game. But you get a code name and a dossier to fill out. You create your fake background—where you were born and how old you are. Then you have to memorize your 'cover.' That's your new identity. When you go through the museum, fake spies ask you questions about your secret identity."

"Awesome!" Luke said, pulling the collar of his jacket up with both hands to mimic an undercover agent. "I've always wanted to be a spy like double-oh-seven."

Quinn continued reading down the page. "Hey, there's even a code name for the president."

"What is it?" M.E. asked.

"*POTUS*," Quinn said. "It's an acronym. It stands for President of the United States. The motorcade that he rides in is called *Bamboo*."

"Bamboo?" M.E. laughed at the funny name. "Where did they get that code name?"

Quinn shrugged. "Listen to this: the vice president's office is called the *Cobweb*!"

The kids giggled at the weird name.

"We're going to be visiting the White House," Cody said. "What's it called?"

"The *Castle*," Quinn answered. "The Capital is called the *Punch Bowl* and the Pentagon is called *Calico*."

"Awesome," Luke said. "Maybe we should give our clubhouse a code name."

Quinn read on. "There's also something in the museum called *Operation Spy* where you get to solve puzzles and read video messages and listen to sound effects—stuff like that. And you can play an interactive game called 'Spy in the City.'"

"Sounds fun. How do you play?" M.E. asked.

"The museum lends you a GPS device and you have to find clues at landmarks around the area," Quinn answered. "Your mission is to discover a password for a secret cache."

"I wonder if we'll get to play." Cody said.

"Mr. Pike said we're going on some kind of Spy Scavenger Hunt and we'll look for coded clues," Luke said.

Quinn put away the small tablet. "I think our homework has something to do with our trip. If you guys want to help Luke and me crack the Washington code that Mr. Pike gave us, we'll help you with the one Ms. Stad gave you."

The girls nodded. Everyone got out pencils. Quinn placed his paper on the floor in front of him so everyone could see it. "Let's race to see who can crack it first."

On the word "Go!" the kids got to work. Cody glanced back and forth between the homework paper and the Washington code she'd copied in her notebook and began translating the message.

∧ ▫ — ⊙    ; ○    < ⌐ ⌐ |·|

+ ⌐ ♯ ?    |· — ⌐ ?

*Code Busters' Key and Solution found on pp. 149, 154.*

Cody was the first one to finish deciphering the coded message, but she waited until the others were done before saying the answer out loud. She didn't want to ruin the fun for them.

"That was easy," M.E. said "And since we belong to the Code Busters Club, we already have code names."

The kids had chosen their own secret identities when they formed the club, and they used their code names when they sent secret messages back and forth. M.E. had used the phonetic spelling of her two initials to create a code name that was also a palindrome. She wrote it down in Washington code:

$$\text{?} \; \square \; \square \; \text{?}$$

Meanwhile, Luke scrambled up the letters of his first name to make it an anagram, then added a rhyming word. He wrote down the coded message. With two repeated letters, he knew it wouldn't be too hard to decipher.

## ⊡⌐?⌐   #⌐#?

Since Quinn's last name rhymed with a spy-type word, he added another word that went with it, which he used for his code name. In Washington Code, it looked like:

## ⊐∟+⊡ & ⊡?<

Finally, Cody used part of her name plus her hair color to create her secret identity. She knew this would be easy to crack but it was fun to create.

## +∟#?   ⊓?#

*Code Busters' Solutions found on pp. 154.*

"Let's write some messages using Washington Code," Quinn suggested. Everyone got out a sheet of notebook paper and began to encode secret messages using the new code. Cody wrote about something she wanted to get at the Spy Museum:

; ∧−∟⊙ −
♯?+∟♯?⊓ ⊓;∟□

Luke thought about why he loved codes so much, then wrote in code the reason:

○=;?○ −⊓? +∟∟⅃

M.E. couldn't think if anything special to say, so she decided to ask a question:

+−∟ <∟⊓ ⊓?−♯
⊙⊡;○

And Quinn decided to make a suggestion for their visit to the Spy Museum and wrote:

⅃?⊙○ ∧?−⊓
♯;○□⅂;○?○

The Code Busters were having so much fun encoding and decoding messages, they lost track of the time. When Cody's cell phone pinged, she read the text from her mother, reminding her to get home.

"Whoa, it's four o'clock. I have to be home in half an hour and we haven't cracked the message Ms. Stad gave us for homework. We better hurry."

Cody set out the homework assignment for the others to see, along with the key to the Japanese code that represented the numbers from zero to nine. The kids hurried to crack the series of numbers that Ms. Stad had written in Japanese.

二三 * 八 * 一五
二三 * 一 * 一四 * 二〇 * 一九
二〇 * 一五
七 * 一五
一五 * 一四
一
九 * 一六 * 二五
八 * 二一 * 一四 * 二〇
?

*Code Busters' Key and Solution found on pp. 149, 154.*

When they were done, M.E. said, "It looks like a bunch of math problems in Japanese. That's not as fun as the Washington Code the boys got."

Was it true? Cody wondered. Had Ms. Stad just given them math problems to do for homework using Japanese characters? She scanned the page, then turned it over and noticed a note in small print at the bottom.

"Look," she said, then read the message to the others: "*Students, when you finish decoding the Japanese numbers, use your Alphanumeric Decoder Card to read the secret message.*"

"Awesome!" M.E. said. "It's actually a coded message, too."

"Dude, maybe it's something about the Spy Museum," Luke offered.

"There's only one way to find out," Quinn said.

The kids got out the alphanumeric decoder cards that Ms. Stad had given them a few months ago and quickly went to work figuring out the message:

23 – 8 – 15     23 – 1 – 14 – 20 – 19

20 – 15    7 – 15    15 – 14    1

19 – 16 – 25    8 – 21 – 14 – 20    ?

*Code Busters' Key and Solution found on pp. 149, 154.*

"This trip keeps getting better and better," M.E. said, after everyone had finished deciphering Ms. Stad's message. "I can't wait to check out the School for Spies and get a Spy vs. Spy T-shirt at the museum! Plus I want to see the National Museum of American History. They've got a collection of old fashions people used to wear."

"I want to see the Apollo 11 Command Module at the Air and Space Museum," Quinn said.

"I'm going to check out the stegosaurus and triceratops fossils at the National Museum of Natural History," Luke added.

"Besides the Spy Museum, I think the Cherry Blossom Festival parade will be—" Cody stopped suddenly. She pressed her finger to her lips, her eyes wide. "Shhh!"

She sat stiff as a board while the others stared at

her. She touched her ear, then shook her hands in front of her—the signs for "hear" and "noise"—then pointed outside. She was certain she'd heard the crack of a twig close by. Someone—or something—was near the clubhouse.

M.E. raised her eyebrows and combed back her hair with her fingers, making the sign for "lion." Cody remembered that hikers had spotted a mountain lion in the area last year, but she and the others had never seen any sign of the wild animal.

Cody cocked her head and listened, waiting to hear the sound again.

After a few seconds, Luke signed the word, "Nothing," by shaping an "O" with his hand.

Cody nodded and started to relax. Luke was probably right. It was nothing.

Anyway, it was time to get home, or she'd get in trouble for being late.

But just as she was gathering up her homework, she heard the sound again—like the crack of a branch underfoot. She could tell from the tense looks on her friends' faces that they had heard the noise this time, too.

There really was someone or something right outside their clubhouse door. And if it was an intruder—or a mountain lion—the Code Busters were trapped.

# Chapter 3

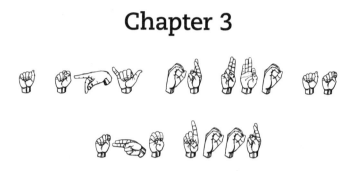

"Hello?" Quinn called through the door.

M.E. rolled her eyes and whispered, "Quinn! If it's a mountain lion, it's not going to answer you."

"I know," Quinn snapped. "I was just trying to scare it off."

"By saying *hello*?"

Quinn frowned at her. "Got a better idea?"

"Dudes, chill!" Luke said. "I'll go see who—or what—is out there."

Cody admired how Luke always stepped up when there was danger. He seemed to be fearless. "But what if it really is a mountain lion?" Cody asked. While she was glad he wasn't afraid, she didn't want him to get hurt.

Luke looked around for something to fend off a possible attack. He pulled up the carpet and opened the secret compartment hidden under the metal floor. It was the perfect place to stash code-busting supplies. So far, they'd collected magnifying glasses, binoculars, flashlights, code books, and a bunch of other cool gear. Luke grabbed the large, heavy-duty flashlight with the long handle and hoisted it up.

"Wait!" Cody said. "I have an idea." She got out her cell phone and opened the sound effects app, then pointed to the air horn icon. "Turn up the volume, then tap this when you get outside. It's really loud. That should scare it away."

Luke kept the flashlight in one hand and took the cell phone in the other, his thumb ready to touch the app.

Quinn unbolted the door and opened it slowly.

Luke stuck his head out.

"See anything?" Quinn asked.

Luke shook his head. He took a step outside, the heavy flashlight raised to swing at an attacker, the cell phone ready to blast. The three other Code Busters peered out behind him, each one holding an object for protection. Quinn had grabbed the plank that blocked the door, M.E. held a pair of scissors that had been hidden in the secret compartment, and Cody was ready to launch a couple of large rocks.

"Shhh!" Cody whispered. She'd heard rustling in the bushes a few yards away. "Over there!" She pointed in the direction of the sound.

Luke tapped the phone app. A loud blast filled the air. He pressed it again and again.

The bushes shook.

Suddenly, a dark shape darted from the back of the bush and sprinted down the hill, through the Eucalyptus Forest.

Luke stopped blasting the air horn and strained to see the running figure. After a moment, he turned to the others behind him. "That was no mountain lion."

"How do you know?" asked M.E., her eyes wide with fear.

"Because mountain lions don't wear extra-large hoodies and saggy jeans." Luke knelt down and picked up something from the ground. When he stood again, he was holding a folded piece of paper. He unfolded it. The page was filled with illustrations. Familiar-looking illustrations, Cody thought.

"And mountain lions don't leave cartoon drawings behind," Luke added.

Cody knew instantly who had been spying on them inside the clubhouse. And who had drawn that picture message that read, "Eye watch ewe."

That wasn't a welcome *sign* at the bottom of the other note. It was a welcome *mat*.

As in Matt the Brat.

\* \* \* \* \*

The Code Busters didn't have time to figure out what the new cartoons meant, so Cody offered to take the paper home, scan it, and email it to the others so they could all work on decoding it later.

With no sign of Matt outside the clubhouse—and no sign of a mountain lion—they jetted down the hill to their homes. Cody, M.E. and Quinn said goodbye to Luke at his condo where he lived with his *grand-mère* (grandmother). Then the girls dropped Quinn at his house across the street from Cody. And finally, M.E. waved goodbye to Cody and continued on to the next block.

"I was beginning to worry," Mrs. Jones said when she saw Cody come in the door. She signed and said the words so that Cody's deaf younger sister, Tana, could be a part of the conversation.

"Sorry," Cody said and signed, circling her chest with a fist. She told her mom and sister about her day, leaving out the threatening notes from Matt the Brat. There was no need to worry her mother any more than she already had.

After a dinner of chicken, green beans, rice, and salad—Cody's favorite meal—Cody helped Tana get ready for bed and read her a story in sign language. Then, Cody brushed her teeth, got into her cat-decorated pajamas, and went to her room to finish her homework. By the time she sat down at her desk, she'd almost forgotten that the second note from Matt the Brat that was still in her backpack.

She pulled it out and quickly scanned it, then emailed the message to the other Code Busters. When she was done, she took a moment to study the drawings. In the middle of the note was a kid in a super hero costume. On each side of him were two kids—two boys and two girls—lying on the ground as if they'd been knocked out. In the background was the logo from the International Spy Museum.

Cody thought the cartoons were really good and wondered why she'd never noticed what a talented artist Matt was. Most of his drawings in class were of monsters, and dragons, and ugly beasts, so Cody never really paid much attention to them. But if he had drawn these cartoons, well, he really had talent. They were amazing—except for the message behind them. It was clear to Cody that Matt the Brat thought he was some kind of super spy. Did he plan to "knock out" the Code Busters at the Spy Museum?

*We'll just see about that,* Cody thought.

* * * * *

The rest of the week couldn't go fast enough for Cody and the other Code Busters. Each day at school their teachers talked about what they'd see and do in Washington, D.C. Mrs. Stad taught Cody's class Washington Code, plus some more Japanese. But Cody had trouble concentrating. She couldn't get her mind off the Spy Museum. There were so many cool exhibits there she was dying to see.

Finally, departure day came. By the time the students boarded the plane at the San Francisco airport, they were all buzzing about what was planned once they reached the nation's capital.

Cody spent the five-hour flight reading a mystery on the mini tablet her mother had let her borrow. Quinn wrote secret messages for the others to solve using the Washington Code key. M.E. watched a movie. Luke mostly slept. Cody checked on Matt the Brat a few times to see if he was up to no good—he was sitting a few rows behind her—but he seemed to be listening to his iPod and drawing pictures. Cody wondered if the Code Busters would be getting more threatening cartoon notes from him during the trip. But if he bothered the Code Busters again, she'd tell Ms. Stad. Her teacher didn't tolerate bullying of any kind.

The view from the plane as it flew into Dulles Airport gave the students a preview of the Cherry Blossom Festival. Clusters of pink blossoms seemed to be everywhere. They reminded Cody of bouquets of pink popcorn. By the time they got off the plane, everyone was excited about the upcoming adventure.

Since the trip had taken most of the day, the students, teachers, and chaperones were bussed straight to the hotel so they could rest up. Still, nobody got much sleep. Everyone was too busy reading the brochures, talking about the sites, and making lists of the souvenirs they wanted to buy.

The next morning, the students woke early, ready for their first stop—The International Spy Museum. Ms. Stadelhofer and Mr. Pike counted the kids as they boarded the bus. When all the students and chaperones were seated, Ms. Stad stood up at the front and clapped to get everyone's attention.

"Good morning, students! Welcome to your first day in Washington, D.C.!

In a few minutes we'll be on our way to the International Spy Museum. A few rules first. Number one, stay with your buddy and stay with the group. Number two, do not leave the Spy Museum for any reason without checking with me. Number three, don't ask your chaperones for help unless you're in trouble. And number four, complete your assignment and turn it in to your teacher or one of the chaperones before you head for the Spy Store. Understood?"

The students nodded and mumbled, "Yes, Ms. Stadelhofer."

"Good. Now, are we ready for the Spy Museum?" she said, grinning.

The classes cheered and clapped. The teachers, along with several parent chaperones, handed out the first assignment sheets to be completed while the students toured the museum. Since the kids were visiting a *spy* museum, naturally the assignment was in code.

"By now, you're all familiar with Washington

Code," Ms. Stad said. "Your assignment is to crack the coded message and follow the instructions. Good luck!"

As the bus headed for the museum, the students began to work on their assignments, deciphering the code.

$$+\sqcap?-\odot?\ -\ \sqcup?\sqcup?\llcorner\#$$

$$\ddagger\llcorner\sqcap\ <\llcorner\sqcap\sqcap\ +\llcorner\sqcap?\sqcap$$

*Code Busters' Key and Solution found on pp. 149, 155.*

By the time they arrived at the Spy Museum, they'd completed their "legends" (fictional spy backgrounds), for their "covers" (secret identities). Cody Jones, aka "Code Red," wrote that she was a Russian spy who moved to the United States to study English. Quinn Kee, aka "Lock & Key," was a US military spy working for Special Ops. M.E. Esperanto, aka "Em-Me," said she was a Mexican national who translated Spanish messages for the United Nations. And Luke LaVeau, aka "Kuel-Dude," claimed he was a soldier and spy during the Civil War.

As they got off the bus and lined up to enter the museum, Cody checked to see where Matt the Brat was, in case he was about to do anything else suspicious that might ruin the trip.

Cody looked down the line but saw no sign of Matt. Maybe he'd gone to the bathroom or had fallen asleep on the bus. At least he wasn't bugging them.

She turned back to her friends who were straining their necks to see inside the museum. She was about to ask if anyone had seen Matt when she noticed a figure standing in an alcove near the entryway. As soon as she spotted it, the figure pulled back into the shadows. All Cody could see were black athletic shoes, the corner of a khaki trench coat, and the brim of a black baseball cap.

Was someone spying on them?

She stepped away from the line to get a better look. Maybe it was someone from the museum, and this was all part of the spy experience.

"Dakota Jones!" Ms. Stad called from the back of the line. "Please stay with your group."

"But Ms. Stadelhofer—" Cody began to argue.

Ms. Stad gave Cody one of her famous looks that clearly said, "Do as I say." Cody frowned and shuffled back into line. She glanced back at the alcove to see if she could catch another glimpse of the person, but from her place in line, she couldn't tell if anyone was still there.

When Ms. Stad wasn't looking, Cody slipped out of line again and moved quickly to the alcove. If some strange person was spying on them, Ms. Stad would want to know, so it was worth the risk of getting caught.

But the alcove was empty. There was no sign of anyone wearing a khaki coat and a black hat. Had she just imagined it? After all, her parents said she had an over-active imagination. And she had spies on the brain. She glanced around to see if Matt was still missing, but she spotted him at the back of the line, so the mysterious person couldn't have been him.

Something lying on the ground inside the alcove caught her eye. She knelt down and picked it up.

It looked like an ordinary ballpoint pen, but Cody was suspicious. It had been lying in the very spot where the stranger stood. She examined it closely but found nothing unusual about it. Pocketing the find, she quickly returned to her place behind M.E. before Ms. Stad caught her again.

"Where'd you go?" M.E. asked.

"I saw something on the ground over there," Cody answered. She pulled the pen out of her pocket to show M.E.

"A pen?" M.E. said.

Cody nodded. She tried clicking the pen, but it didn't seem to work.

"Someone must have dropped it," M.E. said. "Throw it away. It's probably got germs." M.E. was terrified of germs. Not to mention zombies, aliens, mountain lions, the dark, and a bazillion other things.

Cody tried clicking the pen again, but it was still stuck. Curious, she unscrewed the pen and took it apart. *No wonder it doesn't work*, she thought. *The inside parts are missing.*

Just as she was about to throw the pen away, she glimpsed a bit of white. There was something inside. A tiny, rolled-up piece of paper.

Cody pulled it out, unrolled it, and glanced at the symbols written in bold black ink:

; O =< <L⌐

*Code Busters' Key and Solution found on pp. 149, 155.*

The note was written in Washington Code! Cody got out her decoder card and quickly translated the message.

As soon as she did, she felt the hairs at the back of her neck stand up.

# Chapter 4

"Guys," Cody whispered to her Code Buster friends. "I found something weird . . ." She started to show them the note from the pen when a voice interrupted her.

"Welcome to the International Spy Museum," a woman in a black Spy Museum T-shirt and black pants announced to the students gathered in the lobby. "My name is Allison Bishop and I'll be your guide today."

Cody stuffed the pen and note in her pocket. It

looked like they were about to begin the tour. She'd tell the others about the message later.

"The Spy Museum houses the largest collection of international espionage artifacts in the world," Ms. Bishop said proudly. "You'll be able to see everything from lipstick cameras, to tricked-out cars, to overcoats with secret pockets, to shoes with hidden weapons."

Cody spotted a khaki overcoat in a display window nearby. According to the small sign, it was worn by a real spy during the Cold War. To Cody, it looked a lot like the one she'd seen on the figure hidden in the shadow of the alcove.

"As you make your way through the museum, you can read about spies like Mata Hari, who spied for Germany during the World War I, and Aldrich Ames, who worked for the CIA but spied for the KGB. You'll learn about missions like the Red Terror in the Soviet Union and the Manhattan Project that produced the atomic bomb. And you'll learn about the tricks and tools of the trade, everything from hidden lapel microphones to the Enigma cipher machine."

"We have an Enigma machine," Quinn whispered to the other Code Busters. He'd found a broken one at the Army-Navy Surplus Store and bought it for the club.

"You do not!" Matt the Brat blurted. To Cody's surprise, he was standing right behind the Code Busters. There was a sneer on his red, puffy face and his arms were crossed over his extra-large *Plants vs. Zombies* T-shirt. "Those things are top secret. Only the military has them."

Ms. Stadelhofer stepped up and put a hand on Matt's shoulder, reminding him to use a quiet voice. He shrugged her off, but said nothing more. Cody returned her attention to the tour guide, but she could almost feel Matt's dark eyes staring at the back of her neck.

Ms. Bishop continued with her talk. "While you're inside, you'll also learn about spying techniques, such as *dead drops*—secret places where spies exchange information—and *surveillance*—when spies spy on each other. Plus, there are all sorts of hands-on activities, video programs, and interactive computer challenges to experience as you make your way through the museum." She smiled and raised an eyebrow. "Be sure to keep an eye out for counterfeit currency, hidden spy gadgets, and people in disguise."

Cody thought of the stranger in the alcove again. Had it been a staff member wearing a disguise to show them what it was like to be spied on? Was the museum trying to make the visit seem as real as possible? That had to be it.

"For those of you who enjoy spy movies and TV shows," Ms. Bishop added, "check out the props from popular shows like *Mission: Impossible, Spy Kids*, and the James Bond films."

"Bond, James Bond," Luke whispered to the others in a British accent. "Code name: Double-oh-seven." Cody and M.E. giggled.

"The museum is divided into different sections," Ms. Bishop continued after the excited murmuring died down. "In the Covers and Legends area, you can adopt a cover identity. Memorize the information given to you, because you'll be questioned about your cover at some point and you'll need to give convincing answers. Remember: a spy must live a life of lies." She winked.

"Cool!" a boy named Francesco said.

"Sweet!" a few more students echoed.

"We've already got our covers," M.E. told the other Code Busters, "but I'm not a very good liar. My face always turns red and gives me away when I don't tell the truth."

Cody smiled at her friend. It was true. M.E. just couldn't pull off a lie.

"After leaving Covers and Legends, you'll go to the Briefing section," Ms. Bishop continued. "There you'll 'meet' several *virtual* spies. Then, in the School for Spies section, you'll learn what it takes to go undercover. You can check out over two hundred spy gadgets—weapons, bugs, cameras, cars, and other spy-craft necessities. Be ready to be tested on your skills of observation and surveillance. Next, you'll get to create a disguise of your own."

"Awesome!" Luke said. "I hope we get mustaches and those rearview sun glasses."

Ms. Bishop waited until the students settled down again. "That's not all. You'll also get a chance to crack some codes that were used during various wars." She pointed to a large poster on the wall, filled with dots and dashes. "How many of you are familiar with this code?"

All of the students raised their hands except Mika. Ms. Stad and Mr. Pike had taught their sixth graders many codes during the year, including Morse code.

"Wow! I'm impressed," Ms. Bishop said. She held up a large sign written in Morse code. "All right, let's see if you can decipher this message. If you need help, just look at the poster on the wall."

● ━ ━　●　● ━ ● ●　━ ● ━ ●　━ ━ ━　━ ━

━　━ ━ ━

━　● ● ● ●　●

● ● ●　● ━ ━ ●　━ ● ━ ━

━ ━　● ● ━　● ● ●　●　● ● ━　━ ━

*Code Busters' Key and Solution found on pp. 150, 155.*

The students began cracking the coded message. Quinn and Cody were the first to raise their hands when they finished. Ms. Bishop called on Quinn and he recited the answer.

"Great job!" Ms. Bishop said. "Did you know that Morse code was developed in the 1800s by an artist and inventor named Samuel F. B. Morse? He worked with a physicist to create an electrical telegraph system which was used to send encrypted messages between warships, naval bases, and railroads. Sometimes Morse code was used to send distress signals. The most famous one sounds like this." Ms. Bishop gave three rapid knocks on the nearby wall, then three knocks spaced a second apart, then three more quick knocks.

*Code Busters' Key and Solution found on pp. 150, 155*

"Does anyone know what that means?"

Hands shot up. Cody and her friends immediately recognized the distress signal from when Ms. Stad taught them Morse code. Ms. Bishop called on a boy named Ty from Mr. Pike's class.

"S.O.S.," Ty said.

"And what does S.O.S. stand for?" Ms. Bishop asked.

"Save our ship!" a girl named Tessa called out.

"Save our souls!" another boy named Max offered.

"Save our shoes!" Matt the Brat yelled, then laughed at his own joke.

Ms. Bishop ignored Matt's contribution. "Yes, it's come to mean 'save our ship' or 'save our souls'. But do you know what that *really* means?" she asked, grinning.

"HELP!" called out several students, including the Code Busters.

"Correct!" Ms. Bishop said. "S.O.S. is not really an acronym. The letters S and O were chosen because they're easy to use and remember in Morse code— just three dots and three dashes. So, if you're ever in trouble, just tap out S.O.S. and, hopefully, someone will come rescue you!"

Cody heard several students tapping the S.O.S. code on nearby walls.

"All right, everyone," Ms. Stad called out, "Quiet down, please."

Ms. Bishop smiled. "At the end of the tour, you'll get to learn about the history of espionage and how spying was used in the Revolutionary War, the Civil War, and both World War I and II. When you leave the exhibits, you'll have a chance to go to the Spy Store and pick out some spy gear. Once you're finished shopping, find your teachers, because you're going on your very own Spy Hunt mission. In groups, you and your chaperones will explore the Washington Mall seeking out mystery locations with the help of GPS-guided clues."

Once Ms. Bishop finished talking, it was time to get started. Cody and M.E. buddied up. So did Quinn and Luke. Even Matt the Brat had a buddy—a girl named Sadie who was his next-door neighbor.

Cody noticed that the new girl, Mika, was by herself. She remembered what it was like when she was new and didn't know anyone. It took a while to make friends, and she felt lucky to have her Code Busters Club friends.

Cody went over to her teacher. "Ms. Stadelhofer? Mika doesn't have a partner. Can she come with M.E. and me?"

Ms. Stad looked around to see if anyone else needed to pair up, but all of the students had partners. "Well, I suppose she could be my buddy, but she'd probably have more fun with you girls. Thanks, Cody. That's very nice of you."

Mika was standing at the back of the line next to her mother, who was one of the chaperones.

"Hey, Mika. Ms. Stad said you could join M.E. and me if you want."

Mika smiled widely. "Thanks!" She turned to her mother, who nodded, and then followed Cody to where M.E. stood in line.

"Hey! No cuts," Matt the Brat called out from behind them. He gestured with his thumb for Mika to move back. When he held up his hand, Cody noticed his fingertips were black. Yuck!

"She's not cutting," Cody explained. "She's with us and we were already in line."

"I'm telling!" Matt said.

Cody turned to Mika, who was no longer smiling. "Ignore him," Cody said.

Mika nodded, but said nothing.

When the girls reached the entryway, they were handed their dossiers—file folders that held their cover information. Each student received an official-looking ID card with a blank spot for a snapshot, plus spaces to fill in with a fake name, address, and other details. To Cody, the ID card looked a lot like her mother's driver's license, only instead of "State of California" at the top, it read "United States Identification, Department of Secret Activities ."

*Wow,* Cody thought. *Secret Activities?* That sounded pretty official.

Once the students were inside the winding hallways, the Code Busters and Mika explored the exhibits. Quinn was fascinated with all the cameras that were concealed in things like briefcases, wristwatches, and fountain pens. They looked just like ordinary objects—not at all like cameras.

Luke was a big fan of James Bond movies and all the gadgets Double-Oh-Seven used, especially the cars. He always said he wanted an Aston Martin one day. "It's got tire shredders to stop bad guys chasing you, a rotating license plate so you can disguise the car, a bulletproof shield in case someone is shooting at you, and machine guns in the fog lamps if you really need power!"

M.E. was intrigued by the lethal umbrella, which had a sharp point at the tip and could stop bad guys if they got too close, and the lipstick recorder, which looked like a real tube of lipstick, except it could record conversations between two spies. Mika seemed to like all the disguises the spies used, especially the stick-on mustaches and fake glasses. And Cody loved anything that could hide tiny secret messages, like the hollow coin, the concealment ring, the false-heeled shoes, and the fake can of soda. The Code Busters had one of those at their clubhouse where they hid important messages.

When they reached the Spy Shop, the kids headed for their favorite gadgets. After a few minutes, Cody looked around for Mika, but she was nowhere in sight.

Her new friend had gone missing!

# Chapter 5

Cody felt her heart race. The group was supposed to stay together and they'd already lost
one of their members. "Has anyone seen Mika?"
she asked the other Code Busters as she frantically
glanced around the store. "She's gone!"

"She was just here a minute ago . . . ," Luke said,
checking one of the aisles.

"I thought I saw her over there." M.E. pointed
toward the exit.

"We'd better find her," Quinn said.

A kid standing next to Cody turned around and
tapped her on the shoulder. Cody gasped.

"Oh my gosh!" she said. "Mika! I didn't even recognize you!"

Mika had covered her short black hair with a knitted Spy Museum cap and was wearing a black T-shirt over her outfit that read: "A Ninja Swiped My Homework." She'd put on dark glasses, stuck a fake mole onto her cheek, and held a book about spying over her mouth to hide the bottom half of her face.

"Wow, awesome disguise," Luke said to Mika. "How do you like mine?" He stuck a furry black mustache above his upper lip and pulled a camouflage fisherman's hat on his head.

M.E. laughed. "Nice hat, but a mustache? Seriously?"

"I think it looks cool," Luke argued, checking himself out in a mirror.

Following Mika's lead, the other Code Busters began gathering items for their own disguises. Cody found a Russian-style fur hat. "I'm goink to use a *Rr*ussian accent," she said, rolling the letter *R*.

M.E. chose a scarf covered with words like CONFIDENTIAL, FOR YOUR EYES ONLY, and TOP

SECRET, and wrapped it around her head and neck. Quinn found a knitted cap that came with a knitted black beard.

Like Mika, the Code Busters picked out T-shirts to pull over their own shirts. Cody chose DENY EVERYTHING, M.E. picked SPY GIRL, Quinn got a T-shirt with ninjas on it, and Luke found a *Spy vs. Spy* shirt. All five chose dark glasses as a final touch for their disguises.

Ms. Stad called the group to attention. "All right, students, gather your backpacks. It's time for our Spy Hunt. Please pay for your purchases, and then we'll meet in the lobby. I'll assign your group a chaperone, and then each group will receive a GPS unit and the first clue."

Everyone lined up at the cashier to buy their souvenirs and disguises before heading to the lobby. When all the students were assembled, the teachers had them form groups of four and assigned each group a chaperone. The Code Busters got special permission to have five people in their group. Ms. Takeda, Mika's mom, would be their chaperone.

Each chaperone was handed a GPS unit and an envelope with the words TOP SECRET stamped on the front. Cody held the GPS device, which looked a lot like a small hand-held game. The Code Busters had used the GPS apps on their cell phones in the past, so they were familiar with how the device worked.

"You'll find the coordinates on the intel sheets inside your envelopes," Ms. Stad said. "Enter the coordinates into the GPS and begin your mission, then watch for a yellow sign. Good luck. If anyone gets lost or has a problem, your chaperone can call me on my cell phone. We'll meet back here in two hours. The first team to return will get to talk to a real FBI agent, who just happens to be my nephew."

*Awesome!* Cody thought. *We can ask him all kinds of questions about secret missions.*

Quinn opened the envelope that held the first coded message and unfolded the paper. He showed it to the others.

三八° 五三' 二二.○八三七七" N
七七° 二' 六.八六三七八" W

*Code Busters' Key and Solution found on pp. 149, 155.*

The first part was written in Japanese characters. After Mika translated the numbers, the Code Busters quickly solved the code.

"Okay," Quinn said, "we've got the coordinates to find the first waypoint."

"Yeah," M.E. said, "but what's all this other stuff underneath, where it says 'Clue?'"

Luke read the information at the bottom of the page out loud: "There are twelve items buried in the cornerstone here, including atlases, reference books, guides to Washington, D.C., census records from 1790 to 1848, poetry, copies of the Constitution and the Declaration of Independence, and a Bible."

The five kids looked at each other and frowned.

"What's that supposed to mean?" M.E. asked.

"It must be a clue to the waypoint where we're supposed to go," Quinn said.

"Sounds like a cemetery," Luke said. "That's where things are usually buried."

"Yeah, but they bury *people* in cemeteries, not stuff like that," Cody said.

Luke scanned the rest of the clue. "There're also

a bunch of facts about the place." He read the list to the others.

Facts about your destination:

Admission: free

Thickness of walls at the bottom: 18 inches

How many steps: 897

Estimated number of visitors per year: 500,000

Robert mills designed the structure

Obelisk height: 555 feet

Fastest known ascent time: 6.7 minutes

Opened: 1888

Update on damage from earthquake: closed on august 2011

Regulated by: smithsonian institute

Cost to build: $1,187,710

Observation deck via stairs or elevator

Under foundation length: 36 feet

Number of blocks: 36,491

Thickness at top of the shaft: 18 inches

Reason for structure: display of gratitude

Year construction started: 1848, year completed 1884

*Code Busters' Solution found on pp. 155.*

"May I see the paper for a moment?" Mika asked politely.

Luke handed her the sheet. "Does it mean anything to you?" he asked.

Mika smiled. "We have puzzles like this in Japan. Some books are printed so that you read them from top to bottom. Of course, this is in English, not Japanese. But look at the way it's written. Only the first letters of each item on the list are capitalized. *Smithsonian Institute* and Robert Mills's last name are lowercase."

Mika held the paper for the others to see.

"You're right!" Cody said. "That's weird. Our teacher would never make a mistake like that."

"Unless she did it on purpose," Quinn replied.

"Also," Mika continued, "in Japan, we have folding puzzles. I think this is similar. Watch." Mika folded over the right side of the paper until the edge lined up against the first capitalized letters in each of the listed facts.

Cody, Quinn, and Luke's eyes lit up. "Cool!" they said together.

Only M.E. continued to frown at the folded paper. "I still don't get it," she said.

Mika ran her finger down the page to help M.E. see the words that had been hidden in the message. M.E. finally grinned. "I see it!" she exclaimed. "The place we're going to isn't a cemetery at all. Come on! We have to hurry if we want to beat everyone else!"

While she picked up her backpack, Cody glanced at the other groups to see if they had figured out the message, but they all looked confused as they pored over the codes. Good. That meant the Code Busters would be first to reach the waypoint.

Suddenly, Cody felt a chill run down her spine. She had the strangest feeling that someone was watching them. Looking around, she thought she caught a glimpse of the person in the overcoat she'd seen earlier in the alcove. This time she was pretty sure it looked like a man. Was he wearing a mustache? Before she could double-check, he vanished into a shop across the street, so she couldn't be sure.

Cody shrugged. She'd probably imagined it. All this talk of spies and surveillance was scrambling her brain.

Still, she'd keep an eye out for anything suspicious and alert the others if she saw the mysterious man again. If she and the other Code Busters were really being followed and spied on by some stranger, they could be in serious danger.

# Chapter 6

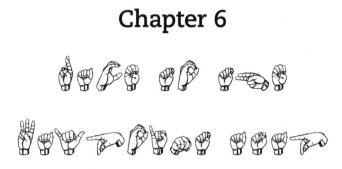

With no sign of the stalker, Cody ran to catch up with the others. Mrs. Takeda stood to the side of the group, quietly listening and watching.

"How do you use a GPS?" Mika pointed to the device in Quinn's hand.

"It's not hard," Quinn said. "We've used our cell phones in a similar way for geocaching."

"What's that?" Mika asked.

Quinn explained, "Geocaching is when you have coordinates—like the ones the teacher gave us—and you enter them into a GPS device. Then the GPS tells you where to find the waypoint—your destination. When we go geocaching, we follow the coordinates to find hidden caches—treasure boxes filled with little things, like dice, or stickers, or magnets, or whatever. You're supposed to take something and leave something for the next group to find."

"Fun," Mika said.

"Yeah," Luke agreed. "It's kind of like a Code Busting treasure hunt."

"How do you work it?" Mika asked.

Quinn held out the device for Mika to see. "First we enter the latitude and longitude numbers to get the waypoint. Then we follow the map to that destination."

"And since we already solved Ms. Stad's clues, we know where to go, so the next hint should be easy to find," Cody said.

The Code Busters headed for the closest Metro station, followed by Mrs. Takeda. Cody noticed that Mika looked a lot like her mom—slim and petite, with short black hair and dark eyes, only

Mrs. Takeda wore glasses. She was good about letting the kids figure out the clues and directions by themselves, while making sure they kept together and stayed safe . . . Still, Cody liked having Mika's mom along. She already saw some of the other parent chaperones telling the kids what to do and practically taking over the game, even though the rules said the chaperones weren't supposed to answer questions. But Mrs. Takeda seemed to know that the Code Busters didn't need—or want—any help.

After a short Metro ride, the kids got off at the Smithsonian station and headed for the Washington Monument. They could see the tall white obelisk, located in the middle of a grassy area and surrounded by flags. A few minutes later, they were in front of the monument and glad to be the first group from Berkley Cooperative School to arrive.

"Whoa, it's so big," M.E. said, craning her neck to look up. "It's like a giant arrow pointing to the sky." The kids gazed at the marble and granite monument that stood over five hundred feet high. Cody noticed the fifty flags that circled the monument, each one representing a state. She immediately recognized the California Bear flag.

"Uh-oh!" M.E. said as she stood near the entrance. "It's closed. I wanted to go up to the top and see all of Washington, D.C."

Quinn peered at the sign. "Yeah, it says the monument was damaged in an earthquake a few years ago and they're still working on it "Well, the next clue has to be hidden around here somewhere," Luke said.

The five kids circled the monument, keeping their eyes out for anything that looked like a coded message. Finally, Mika spotted a yellow sign taped to a nearby post. "I found it!" she shouted to the others.

Cody, Quinn, M.E., and Luke hustled over to where Mika stood pointing. Behind her, Mika's mother grinned proudly at her daughter's accomplishment.

"Way to go!" Luke said.

"Great!" Cody added.

"Yeah," M.E. said, squinting at the encrypted sign. "But guys, we've never seen this code before."

M.E. was right, Cody thought. Their next clue was a complete mystery.

>⊓□ ∟⅃∨>ᴸ□ ⊓⅃∨

>ᒋ⅃ꓶ ⊐ᴇᴇᒋ∨

⊓ᒋ⊐⊐□⊡ ⊃⟨⊡⊡□ᴸ∨

⅃⊡⊐ ∨□∟ᒋ□⟩ ᒋᴇᴇ⊐∨

*Code Busters' Key and Solution found on pp. 150, 155.*

"Now what?" Quinn said.

Mika's mom stepped up to the group. She said nothing, but slowly pulled a manila envelope out of her bag and held it up, smiling mysteriously. Cody looked at the others, then took the envelope from Mrs. Takeda's hand, thanked her, and began to examine it. TOP SECRET was stamped on the outside, along with the words FOR YOUR EYES ONLY, CONFIDENTIAL, and HIGHEST SECU-RITY LEVEL. *This is so fun,* Cody thought as she opened the envelope.

She withdrew a four small decoder cards and a sheet of paper. She passed out the cards, but since there weren't enough, she gave hers to Mika.

"Here are more GPS coordinates for our next waypoint," Quinn said, examining the paper filled with Japanese numbers. "The decoder card must be the key to the new code on the sign. Says here it's called pigpen code."

M.E. giggled at the name. "It looks like a bunch of alphabet letters inside some squares and triangles." Cody looked at M.E.'s card. Some of the letters had dots by them, while others didn't.

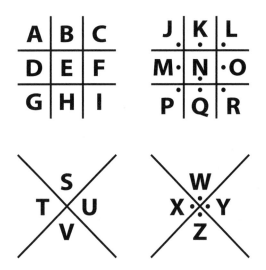

"It's called pigpen?" Luke said. "It looks like more like tic-tac-toe."

"It says here it's also called the Freemason code," Cody said. "Union prisoners in Confederate prisons used the code during the Civil War."

"Okay, Cody and Mika, why don't you two work on the code while Luke, M.E., and I enter the GPS coordinates," Quinn directed. "That'll save some time."

While Quinn, M.E., and Luke used the GPS device, Cody and Mika deciphered the message using the decoder cards. With the key, it didn't take them long to crack the secret message.

"Got it!" Luke announced.

"Us, too!" Mika said.

"Let's go!" Quinn added.

As the kids dashed off, Mrs. Takeda quietly followed them down the gravel path to their next destination. Cody was excited to see the place—code name: The Castle—since she'd seen it in so many movies. One of the Smithsonian museums was also called the Castle, because it looked like a real castle, but the coordinates told them exactly where to go.

She wondered if the president would be there—and what clue they'd find waiting for them. Would it be another Japanese number code? Or would it be in Washington Code? Or maybe this new pigpen code? Cody smiled to herself. With all these codes and clues, Ms. Stad and Mr. Pike had made their trip to Washington, D.C. way more fun than a regular old site-seeing trip. And they'd have plenty of time for that after the Spy Hunt.

When they were about halfway to the White House, Cody put her hand in her hoodie pocket and felt the pen she'd picked up outside the Spy Museum. In her excitement to crack the Spy Hunt codes and find the clues to the next waypoint, she'd forgotten about the pen. But touching it now reminded her of the man in the baseball cap and trench coat.

Had he actually been spying on them? Or was it just her imagination?

She looked around to see if anyone suspicious was watching them. There were lots of tourists walking the mall—groups of school kids like the students from Berkeley Cooperative Middle School, people who spoke different languages, even soldiers in their camouflage uniforms who patrolled the pathways.

It was hard to pick out someone who might be a suspect—kind of like searching for Waldo in a *Where's Waldo* book. But while most of the visitors wore colorful T-shirts, jeans, and hoodies, and were smiling and talking and taking pictures, Cody spotted a lone man lurking by a nearby hot dog stand. She tried to see his face, but it was hidden behind the newspaper he was reading.

She studied him a moment, then realized he was wearing a black baseball cap, a khaki trench coat, and black shoes—just like the guy outside the Spy Museum.

Cody froze and grabbed M.E.'s hand. "Guys!" she called to the others.

Luke, Quinn, and Mika stopped walking and turned around.

"What's up?" Luke asked.

Her eyes wide, Cody waved them closer. Mrs. Takeda stopped behind them, then took a moment to admire a display of T-shirts on a nearby cart while the kids gathered together.

"Why are we stopping?" Quinn asked. "We want to be first, don't we?"

Cody began blinking her eyes.

"What's the matter, Cody?" Quinn asked. "You got something in your eye?"

Cody shook her head, then began the odd blinking again—sometimes fast, sometimes slow.

"Dude, she's blinking Morse code!" Luke whispered to the others.

Cody nodded, then blinked some more. The other watched her eyes intently as she open and closed them at different speeds.

```
—•• ——— —• —
•—•• ——•— ——•— —•—
—•  —•—• •—— —••• ••— —
••  — •••• ••  —• —•—
•—— •  •—• •
—••• • •• —• ——•
••—• ——— •—•• •—•• ——— •—— •  —••
```

*Code Busters' Key and Solution found on pp. 150, 155.*

The kids decoded the message.

M.E. immediately glanced around. "Where?"

"Shh!" Cody hissed, then whispered, "I said *don't* look!"

M.E. turned back to Cody. "Sorry. But who's supposedly following us? And where is he?"

"It's the man I saw back at the Spy Museum," Cody explained. "He was hiding in one of the alcoves outside the building. He was wearing a black baseball cap, a khaki trench coat, and black athletic shoes. I thought I saw him at the Washington Memorial when we were there, too, but he disappeared before I could get a good look. Then I figured it was my imagination. But now I'm sure it's not."

"Where is he now?" Luke whispered. He tried to appear casual as he checked out the area from under his fishing hat.

"Four o'clock," Cody said, using clock position to show the others where the man stood. Four o'clock meant the man was behind and to the right of Cody, if she were looking at a clock.

"Four o'clock?" M.E. repeated before glancing behind her and to the right.

"Not *your* four o'clcok," Cody said. "*My* four o'clock."

M.E. scanned the area. "You mean the hot dog stand?"

Cody nodded.

"Why didn't you just say the hot dog stand?" M.E. said, shaking her head.

Cody sighed. "I wanted to use the clock code."

"Do you guys see him?" Cody said, without turning around. She didn't want the suspect to know she was talking about him.

Luke frowned. Quinn glanced around. M.E. shrugged. Mika looked bewildered.

Cody turned to see why they weren't concerned.

The man in the hat and coat was gone.

A newspaper lay on the ground where he'd stood moments before.

Cody rushed over to the hot dog stand. The others followed.

"Did you see a man standing here a few minutes ago?" she asked the vendor.

"I see many people," the man said, shaking his

head. "You want a hot dog?"

"No, thank you," Cody said, disappointed to hear that the vendor didn't remember seeing the stranger. She stepped over to where the newspaper had been tossed to the ground, knelt down, and picked it up.

"What are you doing?" Quinn asked.

"He was holding this newspaper," Cody said, unfolding it.

"Are you sure?' Quinn asked.

"Yes, I'm sure." She felt a little irritated that the others hadn't seen the man, too. They probably thought it was her imagination, like she had thought earlier. But she hadn't imagined this newspaper. She held it up to read it.

"Kids!" Mrs. Takeda called. She was headed their way and did not look happy. "I thought I'd lost you!" she said when she reached them. "Please don't go wandering off. We need to get to the next waypoint. If you're hungry, I have some crackers in my bag, but we'll be having lunch when we get to the end of the hunt."

Discouraged, Cody was about to toss the newspaper in a nearby trash can, when something caught her eye and she hesitated.

"Wait a second!" she called, as the others began heading toward the second waypoint. "Look at this!"

They turned around.

Cody held up the front page of the newspaper. She hadn't seen it when the paper was folded, but now that it was open, it was so obvious.

There was a hole right in the middle. It went through all of the pages.

The stranger must have torn out small circles about the size of an eyeball so he could spy on the kids while keeping his face covered.

Cody was convinced. They were being followed.

And spied on.

But why?

And by whom?

# Chapter 7

As they continued toward the White House, the kids kept searching for signs of the suspicious man.

"What should we do?" M.E. asked, sticking close to Cody. "Should we tell Mika's mother?"

Cody shook her head. "Not yet. We don't have any real proof. If we see him again, we'll definitely tell her. But be on the lookout. Remember, he's wearing a black baseball cap, a long khaki coat, and black athletic shoes."

"What does he look like?' Quinn asked. "Is he short or tall? Thin or bulky? Did he have a mustache? Was he wearing glasses?"

Cody tried to envision the man. "I think he's about as tall as Luke, maybe taller." Luke was already five feet, eight inches in height, and the tallest member of their group. "And he was on the heavier side. I never really saw much of his face so I don't know if he had a mustache or beard, and he was wearing sunglasses so I didn't see his eyes."

"What color was his hair?" Mika asked. "Black? Brown? Blond?"

"I don't know," Cody answered. "It was hidden under his hat."

"I'm scared," M.E. confessed. "What if he tries to get us? We should tell Mika's mom now before something bad happens."

"Listen," Luke said, "there's safety in numbers. That's why the teachers want us in groups. There's five—no, six of us, counting Mrs. Takeda—so we just have to stay together. That's the most important thing. If anyone spots the guy, use a sign to warn the others so he doesn't know we're talking about him. Then we'll tell Mrs. Takeda and see what she thinks we should do."

"Good idea," M.E. said. "Cody, what sign should we use?"

Cody turned to Mika. "Do you know sign language?"

Mika nodded. "I know a few Japanese signs, but not American Sign Language."

"I'll teach you some," Cody replied.

"First, we should give him a code name, like George Washington and his spies used," Quinn suggested. "Washington's code name was seven-eleven. Why don't we use the same one?"

Since the other Code Busters already knew the numbers in ASL, Cody showed Mika how to count to ten using the manual alphabet as they continued walking along the mall.

"One and two are easy," Cody said, holding up her index finger for one, and two fingers for two. "For number three, you use your thumb and two fingers." She showed Mika the sign by holding up her thumb, index finger, and middle finger. "Four and five are also easy." She held up four fingers, then four fingers plus the thumb for the number five.

"Now it gets tricky. For six, your thumb and pinkie touch." Cody showed Mika by connecting the tips of her thumb and baby finger together. "For number seven, your thumb and ring finger touch. Eight, your thumb and middle finger touch, and nine, your thumb and index finger touch. Zero is just the shape of an O."

"This is fun," Mika said, practicing the numbers as she walked.

"I forget—what's ten?" Quinn asked, holding up the number nine. The others had been practicing their numbers as they walked.

"Shake the letter A with your thumb pointing up," Cody explained. She demonstrated the sign.

"Then what's eleven?" M.E. asked, making the number seven with her ring finger and thumb. "We haven't learned past ten, and Washington's code name was seven-eleven."

Cody held up her index finger and flicked it twice. "Eleven."

While the kids practiced signing "seven-eleven," Cody kept an eye out for the mysterious stranger, aka code "Seven-Eleven." By the time they reached the next waypoint, Mika had the numbers memorized, and the others could sign "seven-eleven" as fast as Cody.

"Anybody see seven-eleven?" M.E. asked when they stopped in front of the White House.

"Nope," Cody said. "Maybe he's off spying on someone else for a change. Why would he *want* to spy on us? We're not real spies, or anything."

"Maybe he works for the Spy Museum, and this is all part of the game to test our powers of observation," Luke offered.

Cody shrugged. She wasn't so sure about that. It seemed like a lot of trouble for a staff member to go to.

"Come on, let's see if we can find the clue," Quinn said, changing the subject back to the spy hunt. "We want to keep our lead." Once again they were the first ones to arrive.

"It's supposed to be right around here somewhere," Luke said. He waved at the area in front of the gate. Moments later he called out, "There it is!"

Luke was pointing to a coded sign similar to the one they'd found at the Washington Monument. This time the message appeared to be in some kind of number code.

7-14-19-16-1     25-3-15-1-21-21-19

17-14-26-25-25-3     1-1-7-19-8     0 0 0

Cody got out her alphanumeric decoder card to see if it might be the key and began translating the message out loud. Moments later she stopped. The decoded message seemed to be a jumble of letters that made no sense. "I don't think this is in Alphanumeric Code," she said. She tried a couple of other codes that used numbers. Nothing worked.

"Mom," Mika called to her mother who was standing a few feet away watching the kids. "Do you have the code key for this message too?"

Smiling mysteriously, Mrs. Takeda stepped up and withdrew another envelope from her bag. Mika grinned. "Thanks!" she said, as she took the envelope it and opened it. She pulled out a sheet of paper covered with alphabet letters and showed it to the group.

"This must be the key," she said, holding up the grid of alphabet letters.

```
a b c d e f g h i j k l m n o p q r s t u v w x y z
b c d e f g h i j k l m n o p q r s t u v w x y z a
c d e f g h i j k l m n o p q r s t u v w x y z a b
d e f g h i j k l m n o p q r s t u v w x y z a b c
e f g h i j k l m n o p q r s t u v w x y z a b c d
f g h i j k l m n o p q r s t u v w x y z a b c d e
g h i j k l m n o p q r s t u v w x y z a b c d e f
h i j k l m n o p q r s t u v w x y z a b c d e f g
i j k l m n o p q r s t u v w x y z a b c d e f g h
j k l m n o p q r s t u v w x y z a b c d e f g h i
k l m n o p q r s t u v w x y z a b c d e f g h i j
l m n o p q r s t u v w x y z a b c d e f g h i j k
m n o p q r s t u v w x y z a b c d e f g h i j k l
n o p q r s t u v w x y z a b c d e f g h i j k l m
o p q r s t u v w x y z a b c d e f g h i j k l m n
p q r s t u v w x y z a b c d e f g h i j k l m n o
q r s t u v w x y z a b c d e f g h i j k l m n o p
r s t u v w x y z a b c d e f g h i j k l m n o p q
s t u v w x y z a b c d e f g h i j k l m n o p q r
t u v w x y z a b c d e f g h i j k l m n o p q r s
u v w x y z a b c d e f g h i j k l m n o p q r s t
v w x y z a b c d e f g h i j k l m n o p q r s t u
w x y z a b c d e f g h i j k l m n o p q r s t u v
x y z a b c d e f g h i j k l m n o p q r s t u v w
y z a b c d e f g h i j k l m n o p q r s t u v w x
z a b c d e f g h i j k l m n o p q r s t u v w x y
```

"Read what it says at the bottom," M.E. said, pointing to the small print. The group huddled together to hear Mika.

"It says, *This is a version of the Confederate Code that was used during the Civil War. Look carefully. The first line shows the alphabet from A to Z. But the second line has shifted over one letter. It begins with the letter B and ends with A. Try to figure out how to crack the code and receive a hint about your next waypoint. Meanwhile, here are the coordinates to the site. Good luck!* It's signed, *E Pluribus Unum*."

Once again, the waypoint coordinates were written in Japanese number characters.

"I've heard of *E Pluribus Unum*," Quinn said. "Those are the words written in Latin on a penny. Mr. Pike told us it means 'Out of many, one.'"

"And what is *that* supposed to mean?" M.E. asked, frowning.

"I think it has something to do with all the American states coming together to form one country—the United States," Quinn said.

"Kind of like *strength in numbers*," Luke noted.

"Okay, let's see if we can crack the code," Cody said. "How about if we match each number to a letter, beginning with the top row."

7-14-19-16-1    25-3-15-1-21-21-19
17-14-26-25-25-3    1-1-7-19-8    0 0 0

*Code Busters' Key and Solution found on pp. 149, 156.*

"The eighth letter is still an *H*," Quinn said.

Luke wrote down the letter *H* in his Code Busters notebook.

"Now let's count over fourteen in the second row," Cody continued. "That gives us the letter *O*."

Luke kept writing down the letters as Cody translated them. Soon they had decoded all twenty-four letters.

Luke read the completed message he'd written down.

"What does that mean?" M.E. asked.

"Like Luke said, it means there's strength in numbers," Quinn said. "But that's not much of a clue to our next waypoint."

"Who said it?" Luke asked.

"I'll look it up." Cody pulled out her cell phone and entered the phrase. A familiar name appeared. "Abraham Lincoln!" she announced.

Quinn looked up from the GPS device. "And guess where the coordinates meet!"

"That makes sense!" Luke said.

"We'd better hurry," Quinn said. "It looks like it's a long way off."

The kids dashed off to find their next waypoint and clue, with Ms. Takeda doing her best to keep up with them. In her excitement, Cody had temporarily forgotten about the man in the khaki coat and baseball cap, but as they neared the steps to the memorial, she stopped and looked around. If she spotted the guy this time, she wouldn't take any chances.

So far, though, there was no sign of him.

Cody felt relieved, but also a little disappointed. Maybe it *had* just been her imagination. Aside from those holes torn in the newspaper, she still had no proof that a strange man was spying on them. Still, if the guy was gone for good, she and the others had nothing to worry about.

Turning her attention to the memorial, she was surprised to see how large it was. She'd seen pictures on the back of pennies and five dollar bills, but nothing prepared her for this. The Lincoln Memorial was built out of marble, surrounded by columns, and decorated with lion heads, wreaths, eagle wings, and the names of the states. But the most impressive sight was Abraham Lincoln in his chair. Over sixty feet high, sixty feet long, and seventy-four feet long, the president was ginormous!

Cody followed the others up the steps to get a better look at the statue of the sixteenth president. She had heard his hands were shaped to represent the ASL letters *A* and *L* so she checked to make sure. She was happy to see the rumor was true!

After pausing to admire the memorial, the kids began searching the area for their next clue. They circled the monument several times before finally gathering at the steps.

"Any sign of the clue?" Cody asked, glancing at the tourists visiting the monument to see if she spotted the stranger.

"Nope," Luke said. "You guys?"

The others shook their heads.

"Mom, do you know where the hidden clue is?" Mika asked as she headed down the stairs to her mother, who was talking on her cell phone.

Mrs. Takeda held up her index finger, signaling, "Just a minute."

Mika waited for her mother, while the others sat on the steps of the memorial.

Suddenly, Mrs. Takeda gasped. She looked pale. Something was wrong.

The Code Busters got up and headed down the stairs to wait with Mika.

"What's up?" Luke whispered to her.

Mika shrugged and stared at her mother.

They stood, listening, but all Mrs. Takeda said was, "No . . . no . . . yes." Moments later, she ended the call.

"What happened?" Mika asked as the others looked on anxiously.

Cody wondered if it might have something to do

with the man she thought had been following them. Had he been trailing the other groups, too? Had he done something? Hurt someone? Had the police caught him?

Mrs. Takeda looked at the kids. "That was your teacher, Mrs. Stadelhofer," she began slowly.

"What did she want?" M.E. asked. "She said we have to stop the hunt and return to the Spy Museum."

"But why?" Quinn complained. "This is fun! We don't want to quit now. We're ahead of everyone else."

Mrs. Takeda took a deep breath. "I'm sorry, kids, but we have to go now."

"Mom, what happened?" Mika pleaded. "Please tell us!"

Mrs. Takeda leveled her eyes on her daughter. "It seems that one of your classmates has gone missing."

"What? Who?" Cody asked.

"A boy named Matthew Jeffreys," Mrs. Takeda replied. "No one has seen him since the Spy Museum tour."

*Whoa!* Cody thought. *Matt the Brat is missing!*

Then she wondered if the man who had been following them had something to do with Matt's disappearance. Maybe she should have said something earlier.

And now it was too late.

# Chapter 8

By the time the Code Busters' group returned to the Spy Museum, most of the other students were already there and on the bus. Cody spotted Ms. Stad standing next to the bus doors, talking on her cellphone. She was frowning and gesturing wildly.

Cody had never seen her teacher look so worried.

She gestured for the other Code Busters to follow her and headed over to see what was going on. Maybe the Code Busters could help. After all, they were great at cracking codes and solving puzzles and finding missing treasure. Maybe they could find Matt.

When they reached Ms. Stad, she ended the call and began talking to one of the Spy Museum security guards. His name tag read "Youngblood."

"The police are on their way," Ms. Stad said to the guard. "Now, are you sure you've searched the entire museum?"

Mr. Youngblood nodded. "Every inch, ma'am. We've called an Adam Alert and closed the museum. No one can get in or out without checking with me or the other guard. Are all of your other students accounted for?"

Ms. Stad looked at her clipboard. "Yes, except . . ." She turned and saw the Code Busters standing next to her.

"Thank goodness your group is here!" she said. "I need you students to get on the bus so I can keep track of you and not lose anyone else."

"What happened to Matt the . . . to Matt?" Cody asked her teacher.

There was no way she would get on the bus without knowing exactly what happened.

"I don't know!" Ms. Stad said, sounding frantic. "Mr. Littlefield, his group chaperone, called me when he noticed Matthew wasn't with the others."

"When was that?" Quinn asked.

"I'm not sure . . ." Ms. Stad shook her head, as if she was trying to think. "According to Mr. Littlefield, Matt began the hunt with his group, but then he ran ahead. Mr. Littlefield called to him to slow down, but apparently Matt ignored him. He figured Matt was excited and wanted to be the first one in the group to the waypoint, but when the others arrived, Matt was nowhere to be found. Mr. Littlefield said they looked for him at the monument, then retraced their steps back here to the Spy Museum, but Matt had vanished."

"I'm sure he'll show up," Cody said, placing a hand on Ms. Stad's arm to comfort her teacher. It was hard seeing her teacher so upset. Ms. Stad was almost always calm, patient, and cheerful.

"Ms. Stadelhofer!" Mr. Littlefield called from the top of the bus stairs. He bounded down the steps. "I almost forgot! One of the kids found this at the Washington Monument. It was sticking out from under the sign post."

The chaperone held up what looked like a brochure for the Spy Museum. He unfolded it and gave it to Ms. Stadelhofer.

"She thought the message was part of the Spy Hunt, but she couldn't make sense of it, so she gave it to me. I stuck it in my pocket and forgot about it when I realized Matt was missing. Do you think it's important?"

Ms. Stad studied the brochure for a moment. The Code Busters leaned over to see what was on it. In the margins were drawings of animals. Cody instantly recognized the artwork—it looked similar to the cartoons she'd found on the paper in her backpack.

Cody pointed to the brochure in Ms. Stad's hands. "They're more drawings. Only this time it's a bunch of animals."

Cody studied the cartoon figures. Their style looked similar to those other pictures they had found during the past week. But there was something weird about them.

"Guys," Cody said to the others, "do you notice anything interesting about these pictures?"

M.E. shook her head.

"What is it?" Mika asked.

"Look," Cody said. "Whoever drew these animals repeated some of them."

"It has to be a code!" Quinn exclaimed.

"That's what I thought," Cody said. "Why would only some of the animals be repeated, unless there was a reason? What if these animals stand for letters, and the repeated ones are double letters?"

"If we can crack the code," M.E. added, "we can figure out what the message says, and maybe find Matt."

Ms. Stad studied the brochure for a moment, then handed it to Cody. "All right, kids, see if you can make any sense of this."

Luke got out his notebook and a pencil.

"Look," Cody said, "there are spaces between some of the animal drawings. Those are probably words. The first word has two tigers, so two of the same letter. They could be *l*'s, *t*'s, *s*'s, *m*'s, *p*'s, *e*'s . . ."

"This could take forever," M.E. muttered.

"Well, we could start with the most common letter

used in English—the letter *E*," Quinn suggested. "That's what real cryptanalysts do. I have a chart in my Code Busters notebook that tells how often certain letters are used in English." He got out his notebook and opened it to the page that was headed, "Letter Frequency."

Quinn pointed to the next letter. "The next is *T*, then *A*, then *O*, then—"

"And *that* could take forever, too!" M.E. complained again.

"Got a better idea?" Quinn asked her.

M.E. shrugged.

Cody glanced over at her teacher, who was talking with both security guards.

"Guys," she said, holding up her hand. "If this code was written by Matt and left for the others to find, then I'm guessing it's pretty simple. Think about it. He didn't use any of the codes we've learned in class. He used drawings. The first one is a picture of a mouse."

"Yeah," Luke said, "and the second one is a monkey."

"An ape, actually," Mika offered. "Monkeys have tails and are smaller than apes."

"Okay, an ape," Cody confirmed. "And the last two are tigers. I think I know what he was trying to do."

"What?" M.E. asked.

"Remember that code we had earlier where the first letters spelled the answer to the puzzle?" Cody asked.

The others nodded. "Yeah, 'Father of The Country,'" Luke said.

"So what letters do each of these animals' names start with?" Cody asked.

"Oh," M.E. said, her face lighting up. Everyone grinned as they finally understood how to crack the code.

Cody said each letter aloud, then Luke wrote them down. When he was done, he read the message to the group.

"Matt the Brat thinks he's James Bond!" M.E. said, rolling her eyes.

Cody handed the brochure back to her teacher.

"We solved the code," she said, proudly, and told her what it said.

*Code Busters' Solution found on p. 156.*

Ms. Stad nodded, but she didn't look pleased. "But I'm afraid it doesn't tell us where Matthew is. You kids need to get on the bus now. I don't want to have to worry about you, too."

"How about if we look for him?" Cody suggested. "You know the Code Busters are good at solving mysteries. This is a mystery. And besides, we sort of know how Matt thinks."

Ms. Stad gave a weak smile at Cody's suggestion. "That's very nice of you, kids, but I can't take the chance that you'll end up missing, too. Now, please, have your group get on the bus. It looks like the police are here and I need to speak with them."

A patrol car had pulled up in front of the museum. Two officers got out of the black and white police car. They would have looked intimidating to most kids, with their official uniforms and all that police gear hanging from their belts. But Cody's mom was a police officer, so Cody was used to cops.

While Ms. Stad was distracted, Cody sneaked over to the alcove where she'd seen the stranger lurking earlier. It was empty. Cody wondered if the stranger had something to do with Matt's disappearance.

"What if Matt's causing all this trouble just so he can win the Spy Hunt by himself?" Luke suggested as Cody returned to the group. "After all, he thinks he's some kind of kid James Bond."

"Yeah," M.E. agreed. "He'd do just about anything to beat the Code Busters at something like this. Except play fair and do the work."

"But why would he care so much about beating you?" Mika asked.

M.E. shrugged. "Who knows? From the minute we formed the Code Busters Club, he's tried to break into our clubhouse, intercept our secret messages, find our drop zones, and steal our Code Buster notebooks."

"Maybe he just wants to be a part of the club," Mika suggested.

The four Code Busters stared at Mika, then looked at each other.

"She could be right," Cody said, shrugging. "I don't like Matt, but I do feel sorry for him. He doesn't have a lot of friends."

"That doesn't mean we'll let him into the club!" Quinn protested.

"No," Mika said slowly, "but maybe you can think of some other ways to include him. I know what how it feels to not be included in things."

Cody smiled at Mika and wondered if she still felt like an outsider at Berkeley Cooperative Middle School. "You have a point," she said. "And maybe if we're a little nicer to Matt, he won't bother us so much."

"I wish Ms. Stad would let us help her find Matt," Cody said.

"Me, too," said M.E. said.

"Dude," Luke said, nodding toward Ms. Stad. The teacher was gesturing wildly as she talked to the police officer. "Look. She's pretty distracted right now." Cody saw a twinkle in his eye.

"Yeah," Quinn added, "she doesn't seem all that interested in us at the moment."

"What are you thinking?" M.E. asked.

Luke glanced around to see if anyone was in earshot. He decided not to take the chance of someone overhearing him, so he began to wave his arms around, as if he were stretching, only in an odd way. Cody, Quinn, and M.E. immediately knew what he was doing—sending them a message in Semaphore Code, using his arm positions to form letters.

*Code Busters' Key and Solution found on pp. 151, 156.*

# Chapter 9

"I'm not so sure that's a good idea," M.E. whispered. "Ms. Stad wants us to stay here."

Mika looked confused. Cody realized she didn't know semaphore code, so she whispered the translation in her ear. Mika nodded, then said "Shouldn't we just let the police search for Matt?"

"We know what he looks like better than the cops," Quinn said. He glanced around, then leaned over to Cody and whispered, "Uh-oh. Sierra Tango Alpha Delta . . . Charlie Oscar Mike India November Golf . . . Tango Hotel ndia Sierra . . . Whisker Alpha Yankee."

*Code Busters' Key and Solution found on pp. 152, 156.*

The others quickly decoded the phonetic alphabet code—all except Mika, who looked bewildered at the odd-sounding language.

"Tango Hotel India November Kilo . . . Foxtrot Alpha Sierra Tango!" Quinn added, in case their teacher was close enough to overhear him.

*Code Busters' Key and Solution found on pp. 152, 156.*

Cody nodded. She had an idea. She only hoped Ms. Stad would go for it.

"Students!" Ms. Stad said as she came up behind Cody. Her arms were crossed over her chest, and she didn't look very happy. "I thought I told you all to get on the bus. What's the problem?"

Cody took a deep breath and spoke up. "I know you said to join the rest of the class, Ms. Stadelhofer, but we think we know how to find Matt. He's been leaving clues like the ones on that brochure, and we think we figured out what they mean. Plus, we have an idea where he may be headed next. Could we please try to find him ourselves?"

"Absolutely not!" Ms. Stad said. "Now—"

Cody cut her off. "Of course, we'd want our

chaperone, Mrs. Takeda, to come with us. I know she'll make sure we're safe." Cody sent Mrs. Takeda a look. Mika's mom smiled back.

Ms. Stad bit her lip. Cody could tell her teacher was thinking over her suggestion. Ms. Stad knew the four Code Busters Club members were smart. In the past, they'd uncovered the answers to several tough puzzles and, in the process, had helped save an elderly man, uncovered stolen diamonds, found hidden treasure, and stopped a museum thief. Cody also knew their teacher wouldn't just let them go running around the Washington Mall by themselves, no matter how smart they were.

Guessing that Ms. Stad was on the verge of agreeing to the plan, Cody added, "And if we get into any trouble—which we won't—Mrs. Takeda can help us, or call you."

Mrs. Takeda stepped forward. "I'd be happy to go with them," she told the teacher. "These kids do seem to have a knack for solving puzzles. They were in the lead during the Spy Hunt. I think they just might be able to find your missing student."

The Code Busters smiled at Mrs. Takeda. Mika beamed with pride.

"All right, all right!" Ms. Stad said. She suddenly looked tired and Cody felt sorry for her. *It must be awful to lose a student you're responsible for,* she thought. That made it all the more important that the Code Busters find Matt the Brat.

"But I want you to check in every fifteen minutes and let me know where you are and what you've found, understand?" Ms. Stad ordered.

"Yes, ma'am!" they all said. Mrs. Takeda nodded.

"Don't make me regret this," Ms. Stad added, giving them a stern look.

"We won't, we promise," M.E. said. She was clearly excited to be a part of the hunt for the rogue spy.

"So what's your plan?" Ms. Stad asked.

"We think Matt's trying to finish the Spy Hunt on his own and then claim he's the winner, so we're going to do the same thing," Cody said. "But first we'll need the list of all the waypoints."

Ms. Stad reached into her vest pocket. She blinked several times as she rooted around with her hand.

She tried the other pocket. Then she searched the pockets of her slacks.

"Oh my goodness!" she exclaimed. "The master list of waypoints is gone!"

Cody glanced at the others. She slowly finger-spelled four letters:

*Code Busters' Key and Solution found on pp. 151, 156.*

Quinn, Luke, and M.E. nodded. Somehow, their troublesome classmate had stolen the list from Ms. Stad's pocket. No wonder he knew where to go so quickly. He didn't have to figure out any of the clues or coordinates. And that was why he'd always been a step ahead of the Code Busters.

Cody thought for a moment, then asked, "Ms. Stadelhofer, do you have a list of the clues? Or even the coordinates?"

Ms. Stad shook her head. "My whole master list is gone. I'm afraid you'll have to go to each waypoint from the beginning to solve the clues and get the coordinates before you can move on to the next one.

That's going to take time." Ms. Stad's face clouded over with worry. "I'm not so sure this is a good idea after all."

"No problem," Cody said, trying to cheer up her teacher. "We can do it, right, guys?" She glanced at the others. They nodded, although M.E. suddenly didn't look so sure. "Come on. We'd better get going." *Before something bad happens to Matt and he ends up lost forever!*

Ms. Stad turned to Mika's mom. "Mrs. Takeda, you have the envelopes with the clues. Would you please give them to the group?"

Mrs. Takeda reached into her purse and withdrew a handful of unopened envelopes.

"Now, if they don't find Matthew within an hour," Ms. Stad continued, "then I want the students back here—safe and sound." She turned to the kids. "Please listen to Mrs. Takeda. If she thinks there's a problem, you are to return to the Spy Museum immediately. No arguments, understand?"

This time it was the Code Busters' turn to solemnly nod.

"Here you go, students," Mrs. Takeda said, handing them the last three envelopes. They were numbered 3, 4, and 5. Cody took them, kept the one numbered 3, and put the other two in her backpack. She ripped open the envelope and gave the coordinates to Mika, who translated the Japanese numbers for Quinn. Then Quinn and M.E. went right to work with the GPS device to locate the next waypoint.

Meanwhile, Cody and Luke worked on the code. Cody thought it would be easy to decipher, since it was in LEET code. The message looked sort of like it was made up of letters of the alphabet, but the letters were created out of numbers and keyboard symbols. It still took them a few minutes to figure out what the message said, since some of the words were unfamiliar to the girls.

4 |_ |_ 0 $ 4 (_) |2 (_) $     /\/\ 3 |) ! (_) $

( 3 |2 4 + 0 $ 4 (_) |2 (_) $     /\/ 4 $ ! ( 0 |2 /\/ ! $

$ + 3 6 0 $ 4 (_) |2 (_) $     $ + 3 /\/ 0 |* $

+ |2 ! ( 3 |2 4 + 0 |* $     4 |_ + ! ( 0 |2 /\/ ! $

*Code Busters' Key and Solution found on pp. 152, 156.*

"That was harder than I thought it would be," Cody complained. "I only recognize a couple of the words, like stegosaurus and triceratops. What do you think it means?"

"We'll have to wait for Quinn and M.E. to give us the waypoint," said Luke, "but I'm guessing we're going to the National Museum of Natural History."

"Why there?" Cody asked.

"That's where the dinosaurs hang out," Luke answered.

Quinn and M.E. soon confirmed the waypoint, pinpointing the museum on the GPS, then locating it on their cell phone map.

"Let's go!" Luke said.

Using the Metro again, the kids headed back to the mall, with Mrs. Takeda trailing behind. The National Museum of Natural History was only a short walk from the Metro stop, so they ran, with Mrs. Takeda doing her best to keep up with them on her high heels. Everyone was out of breath by the time they reached the large cement building topped with a giant dome and flanked by columns.

According to the Internet, the museum, which housed dinosaur bones, was one of the most popular sites in Washington, D.C. Luke had been looking forward to seeing them, but he'd have to wait to view the reassembled fossils until Matt was safe.

"I wish we could go inside," Luke said as they searched the area for the next coded sign. "There's supposed to be like fifty different dinosaurs there—Allosaurus, Triceratops, Stegosaurus. I have a whole collection of dinosaur models I made out of kits. They were like putting puzzles together."

"We'll come back. Don't worry," Cody said. "But right now, we've got to find the next clue."

While Mrs. Takeda sat down on a nearby bench and slipped off her high heels, the kids searched the front of the building.

Cody suddenly thought she saw someone in a trench coat and baseball cap. She was about to alert the others when she realized the guy's hat wasn't black—it was dark blue. She glanced at his shoes. They were white. *Mistaken identity*, Cody told herself. She was letting this hunt go to her head.

Moments later, Luke called, "I found it!"

The group rushed over to the far side of the museum doors, where Luke stood staring at the cryptic sign, written in the phonetic alphabet code, used by NASA.

*Hotel Echo Romeo Echo*
*Yankee Oscar Uniform Lima Lima*
*Foxtrot India November Delta:*
*Romeo Oscar Charlie Kilo*
*Mike Oscar Delta Uniform Lima Echo*
*Sierra Papa India Romeo India Tango*
*Papa India Oscar November Echo Echo Romeo*
*Foxtrot Romeo India Echo November Delta Sierra*
*    Hotel India Papa*

Code Busters' Key and Solution found on pp. 152, 156.

Cody was puzzled by the clue and the code.

"What's it supposed to mean?" M.E. asked.

Quinn smiled mysteriously. "A *rock*, a *module*, a *Spirit*, a *Pioneer*, and *Friendship*. I know what the words mean."

"Really? What?" M.E. asked.

"Well, think about it," Quinn said. "What do they all have in common? If you add the word *moon* to *rock* and you get *moon rock. Module?* How about *lunar module?* The *Spirit* of St. Louis—Charles Lindberg's airplane. The *Pioneer* was a space probe. And there was a spacecraft called the Mercury *Friendship.*"

"They all have to do with space!" M.E. cried. "That's the next waypoint."

"The Air and Space Museum, to be specific," said Quinn.

"Great job!" Cody said to Quinn. No wonder Quinn had cracked the code. He had set up a scale model of the planets in his bedroom, and had painted glow-in-the-dark constellations on his ceiling.

"Well, what are we waiting for?" Quinn said.

They waved to Mrs. Takeda to follow them. Cody looked back to make sure she was coming and saw their chaperone slip on her shoes and rise from the bench. Then the Code Busters and Mika checked their map to see where the Air and Space museum was. Seconds later, Cody and the others heard a scream.

They turned around to see Mrs. Takeda lying next to the bench. Her right foot was twisted at an odd angle. Cody noticed the heel of one shoe had broken off and was stuck in a crack in the concrete.

*"Mom!"* Mika yelled. She ran back to her mother and knelt down. The kids followed her and huddled around their chaperone. "Mrs. Takeda, are you all right?" Cody asked.

Mrs. Takeda moaned and shook her head.

"I . . . think I've broken my ankle," she said, pain evident in her face. "I don't think I can walk!"

Mika's face clouded over. *"Tasukete!"*

Cody didn't need to speak Japanese to know what Mika meant.

*Help!*

# Chapter 10

"Oh no!" M.E. cried. "Now what do we do?"

"We get Mrs. Takeda help," Cody said, taking charge. She pulled out her cell phone and called the number Ms. Stad had given the students in case of an emergency.

Her teacher answered immediately. "Hello?" she said, sounding anxious.

"Hi Ms. Stad. It's Cody."

"Did you find Matt?" Ms. Stad asked.

"Not exactly," Cody said. "I'm calling about Mrs. Takeda. She fell and hurt her ankle."

Cody heard a gasp at the other end of the line. "Is she okay?"

"I don't know. She can't walk and she's in a lot of pain."

"All right, where are you?"

Cody told her that Mrs. Takeda had caught her heel in a crack on the steps at the National Museum of Natural History and had fallen. She glanced over at the chaperone and saw Mika holding her mother's hand.

"What should we do?" Cody asked her teacher.

"I'll call for an ambulance," Ms. Stad said. "You kids just stay put. I'll send Mr. Littlefield to escort you back here."

"But we haven't found Matt yet," Cody protested.

"We'll just have to leave that to the police now," Ms. Stad replied, her voice firm. "I want you students safe and accounted for. I should never have let you go. Now, here's Mr. Littlefield's cell phone number, just in case you need it."

After Ms. Stad gave her the chaperone's number, Cody hung up, then told the others what Ms. Stad had said. The kids sat down glumly on the steps next to Mrs. Takeda to keep her company while they waited for the ambulance and Mr. Littlefield.

"Great," Quinn mumbled, hanging his head. "We didn't find Matt and we didn't get to finish the hunt."

"I'm so sorry, kids," Mrs. Takeda said. She looked like she was in serious pain, and Cody wished she could do something for her.

"It's not your fault," Cody reassured her.

"No," Quinn said, "It's Matt the Brat's fault for causing all this trouble."

The kids grew silent, discouraged because the hunt was over and they hadn't completed their real mission—finding Matt. Several tourists stopped to see if they could help the injured Mrs. Takeda, but the kids explained that emergency medical techs were on the way. It wasn't long before an ambulance drove up, lights flashing. Two uniformed EMTs jumped out and rushed over to Mrs. Takeda.

The kids watched as the female EMT gently examined Mrs. Takeda's ankle, then asked her to move her foot, which made Mrs. Takeda wince.

"She may have a broken ankle," the woman said when she was finished. The two EMTs gently lifted Mrs. Takeda onto a waiting gurney. "We're going to take her to Washington Hospital." She looked around. "Is there another adult coming for you kids?"

"Yeah," Quinn said. "Our teacher is sending someone. We'll be all right until he gets here."

The EMT frowned. "I don't like leaving you here alone, but we've got to get her to the hospital. Stay here, stick together, and wait. Don't go wandering off."

The kids nodded.

The male EMT pushed the gurney into the back of the ambulance. Mika stepped over to him and asked, "Can I come with her? She's my mother."

"Of course," the man said.

Mika looked at the Code Busters. "Will you guys be okay?"

"Sure," Cody said, speaking for the group. "You need to be with your mom. I'll tell Ms. Stad you've gone with her to the hospital. Thanks for all your help."

"Sorry we didn't find Matt," Mika said. Then she climbed into the back of the ambulance to join her mother. Moments later they drove off.

The Code Busters sat down on the steps again. Cody texted Ms. Stad that Mika had gone with her mother to the hospital. Quinn sighed loudly. "Well, I guess we just have to wait until Mr. Littlefield gets here, then go back to the Spy Museum and get on the bus."

They waited in silence for a few minutes, lost in their own thoughts. Suddenly, a strange movement caught Cody's eye. She thought she saw someone duck behind one of the marble columns that flanked the Natural History Museum's entrance. Leaning over to see better, she spotted the toe of a black shoe just peeking out.

*Why would someone be hiding behind that column?*

Cody froze. Her breath caught in her chest.

Was it the stranger who'd been following them? Had he caught up to them? If so, they could be in real trouble.

Slowly she turned to the others and made the sign for the number seven, followed by the number eleven. She kept her hand low so only the Code Busters could see her hand. Luke sat up and looked around. Quinn frowned. M.E.'s eyes widened.

"Where did you see him?" Luke whispered, his eyes darting around the area.

Cody signed the number three, then tapped her wrist, indicating "Three o'clock" on a clock face.

The kids looked to the side of Cody. Just at that moment, the figure peered out from behind the column. He wore a black baseball cap, khaki trench coat, black shoes, and was holding a newspaper over his face.

The newspaper had a hole in the middle of it.

Cody was right. It *was* the stranger who had been following the Code Busters!

"I see him!" Luke whispered, excited.

"You were right!" Quinn said. "We *are* being followed!"

"Should we call the police?" M.E. asked, scooting closer to Cody. She looked terrified.

Before Cody could answer, the stranger threw down the newspaper, turned around, and fled.

"Dude, he's getting away!" Luke said, bolting up.

"We need to follow him and find out who he is and what he's up to," Quinn said, rising to his feet.

M.E. shook her head. "We're supposed to stay here! That's what Ms. Stad said. If we leave, we'll really get in trouble."

Cody knew they had to think fast or they'd lose the opportunity to catch this guy. But M.E. was right. They'd be in big trouble for leaving without a chaperone.

And what if the stranger turned out to be dangerous?

"*E Pluribus Unum!*" Luke called out.

The others looked at him as if he were crazy.

"What?" M.E. said.

"*E Pluribus Unum,*" Luke repeated. "Remember what it means?"

"*Out of many, one,*" M.E. answered. "So?"

"Listen, if we stick together as one, there's

safety—and strength—in numbers," Luke explained. "I say we go after him."

"But the chaperone . . ." M.E. whimpered.

Cody kept an eye on the stranger while the others decided what to do. As the guy was about to turn a corner, she said, "Luke, M.E., Quinn—watch him. I'll text Mr. Littlefield and let him know where we're going."

"Write it in LEET code," Quinn suggested as the two boys began heading in the direction of the stranger. "Just in case there are any spies hanging around. You never know."

"But will he understand it?" Cody asked.

"Oh yeah. He's a computer engineer."

Quickly, she text Mr. Littlefield a coded message.

$ () |2 |2 \|/   \/\/ 3   # 4 |)   + ()   |_ 3 4 \/ 3
\/\/ ! |_ |_   3 * |* |_ 4 ! /\/   |_ 4 + 3 |2

*Code Busters' Key and Solution found on pp. 152,156*

"Hurry!" M.E. called back to Cody as she followed the boys.

When Cody was done, she ran to catch up with the others. She was nearly out of breath when she reached them. "Did you lose him? Where did he go?"

"In there," Luke said, pointing to the entrance of the National Sculpture Garden. It was located next door to the Natural History Museum.

"Come on!" Quinn said. "Let's go after him!"

# Chapter 11

CODE: FIND THE
SCULPTURE!

As the kids reached the entrance to the Sculpture Garden, they paused to look around for any sign of the guy in the trench coat. There were lots of tourists walking around in the area, but the stranger seemed to have vanished.

"We've lost him!" M.E. cried out.

"Dude, he could be anywhere!" Luke exclaimed.

"Now what?" Quinn asked, crinkling up his nose.

Cody's eyes lingered on one of the sculptures near a fountain. It looked like a giant rabbit sitting on top of a rock. The rabbit's head was on his fist, as if he were thinking.

She thought she'd seen someone duck behind it.

"I think I spotted him," Cody whispered to the others.

"Where?" Quinn asked, searching the area.

"See that rabbit-looking thing on that big rock?"

"Yeah," Quinn said, squinting at it.

"Don't stare at it!" Cody warned. "Act casual. I think he might be hiding behind it."

"Should we call the police?" M.E. asked.

"Not yet," Cody answered. "We need to get a good look at him first. Then we'll call them."

"What about Matt?" Quinn asked. "We still have to try to find him."

"We will, as soon as we check this guy out," Cody said. "And after we call the police, we'll head for the next waypoint—the Air and Space Museum—and see if Matt's there."

The others nodded. Quinn got out his cell phone, ready to call 911, while Luke looked around for someone in charge, like a security guard or a docent.

M.E. trailed behind the group as they headed for the rabbit sculpture.

"Act normal," Cody reminded the Code Busters. They began pointing out the other sculptures nearby—a giant spider, a running stick man, a bunch of stacked chairs.

But as soon as they got close to the rabbit statue, the stranger in the trench coat shot out from behind it and started running through the grounds.

"There he goes!" Quinn said.

"After him!" Luke yelled. "Don't let him get away!"

The boys took off running. The girls were right behind them. The stranger led them through the winding pathways, past a bunch of weird pieces of art: red arches, an old-fashioned eraser, a robot. Cody wondered what the Code Busters would do with the guy if they actually caught him, but she figured she'd worry about that if and when they did.

"He's heading out of the garden!" Luke called, pointing to the figure dashing for the exit.

"Now where's he going?" M.E. asked, panting from all the running.

"I don't know," Luke answered, "but we can't lose him now. We're right behind him."

As soon as they got to the street, the man seemed to vanish into the crowd. The Code Busters stood on the corner, checking all directions, hoping to catch sight of the stranger again.

"Great. We lost him," Quinn said, shoving his hands into his pockets. "We'll never get this guy, even though he keeps showing up everywhere we go. What does he want?"

Cody shrugged. "We might as well go to the next waypoint and see if we can find Matt."

Cody checked her phone for a return text from Mr. Littlefield, but there was nothing. The Code Busters headed for the Air and Space Museum, hoping they'd find Matt when they got there—or at least another clue as to where he might be. By the time they reached the super modern-looking building, Cody felt discouraged. There was no sign of Matt or the stranger who'd been following them.

"I wish we could go inside," Quinn said, looking up at the needle sculpture in the front of the building.

"Ms. Stad said we're going there tomorrow," Cody answered.

M.E. shook her head. "That's if we find Matt. If we don't, the whole trip will be ruined. We'll probably have to go home."

"Dude, we'll find him," Luke said. "Come on, let's see where the clue is. We're running out of time."

While the others searched for the yellow sign with the clue, Cody texted Mr. Littlefield to let him know where they were. She thought it was odd that he hadn't responded yet. Hadn't he figured out her code? Maybe he was just too busy to respond.

4 + + # 3  4 ! |2 4 /\/ |)  $ |* 4 ( 3  /\/\
(_) $ 3 (_) /\/\ ,  0 /\/ 3  /\/\ 0 |2 3 \/\/
4 \|/ |* 0 ! /\/ +  + 0  6 0 , + # 3 /\/  \/\/
3  \/\/ ! |_ |_  8 3  8 4 ( |<

*Code Busters' Key and Solution found on pp. 152, 157.*

She waited for a moment, but got no reply. Cody thought about texting Ms. Stad, but she didn't want to upset her teacher. She saw Luke waving at her frantically. It looked like he had found the next message. Cody ran up to meet the others.

"What does it say?" she asked, hoping they had already deciphered the code.

"See for yourself," Luke said, pointing to the list of words on the sign. The message was written in Washington Code. Quinn got out his Code Busters notebook and together the kids translated the symbols into letters and words.

$$\mp \, ; \, \# \, ? \, \sqsupset \, ; \, \odot <$$

$$| \, \sqcap \cdot \, - \, \urcorner \, ? \, \sqcap \cdot <$$

$$; \, \llcorner \, \odot \, ? \, \square \, \sqcap \cdot \, ; \, \odot <$$

*Code Busters' Key and Solution found on pp. 149, 157.*

Cody read the completed message aloud, then frowned. "What's it supposed to mean?"

"Good question," M.E. said, shrugging.

Although Cody knew what the words themselves

meant, she wasn't sure why these three words were grouped together. She got out her cell phone and keyed in each word to find its definition. Maybe that would offer a clue.

"The first word means being loyal or faithful," Cody told the others. "The next word means having courage. And the last word means being moral and ethical, like doing the right thing."

"That's supposed to be the clue?" M.E. said, shaking her head. "I still don't get it. And without the waypoint coordinates, how are we going to find the next place?"

"Wait a minute," Luke said. "Maybe the clue isn't the words, but what's *in* the words."

"You mean like a hidden code within a code?" Quinn asked.

"Yeah, like, the *i*s could be dots and the *t*s could be dashes for Morse code," Luke said. "Like *i i t i t i t* could be *dot dot dash dot dash dot dash*."

They tried several combinations on paper using Morse code, trying to make letters and words out of dots and dashes, but nothing worked. Luke shrugged. "It still makes no sense."

"Maybe it's simpler than that," Cody suggested. "Look how the first letters in each of the words is a little larger than the others."

"Like they're capitalized?" M.E. asked.

"Maybe," Cody said. She studied the words and letters a few more seconds. Suddenly the answer jumped out at her. "I've got it! Look at the first letters of each word!"

"Dude!" Luke said. "It's so obvious now!"

"Let me check the address," Quinn said. He used his cell phone to find the information. "It's 935 Pennsylvania Avenue. That's pretty close to the Spy Museum," he said, checking his map app.

"Well, if we don't find Matt there, we'll have run out of waypoints. Game over," M.E. said.

"Then we just have to make sure we do find him!" Cody answered.

# Chapter 12

As they neared the J. Edgar Hoover FBI building, Cody hoped they'd get a chance to go inside sometime. She remembered reading about the place. It sounded like a whole city rather than just an office building. Inside, there was supposed to be a car repair shop, a basketball court, a cafeteria, a roof garden, a cryptographic vault, a photo lab, an exercise room, a firing range, a medical clinic, and even a morgue. The morgue sounded kind of creepy. There were also supposed to be glass windows so people could see the FBI agents actually working. *How cool would that be?*

The building was massive, made out of concrete, with lots of opaque windows. Cody thought it looked more like a prison than a federal agency. She wondered what it would be like to be a special agent and work there. It would be fun hunting criminals, spying on bad guys, and doing all that forensic work like she'd seen on that CSI show her mom sometimes watched.

The Code Busters began exploring the front of the building, searching for the next coded sign. The corner entrance looked more like a movie theater, but with an American flag where the name of the movie would normally be. Not spotting anything there, they headed down the right side of the building and searched some more. Again, they found nothing.

"You guys!" said M.E. "I just thought of something. Remember when we were trying on disguises in the Spy Museum store?" The others nodded.

"I saw Matt trying on a bunch of different things. He kept looking at me, and I thought that was strange."

"Can you remember what he bought?" Cody asked.

"I think he got sunglasses—the kind where you can see behind you. And he was looking at fake mustaches, but I don't know if he got them or not.

Cody frowned. "Wait a minute. The guy who's been following us had sunglasses and a mustache."

"Exactly," said M.E. "I think the stranger is Matt."

The Code Busters stared at each other. Was that possible?

"But he also had on a baseball hat and a khaki coat, so it couldn't have been Matt," said Quinn.

"Why not?" Luke asked. "Maybe he brought along the hat and coat in his backpack."

"Because he wears those dirty white athletic shoes without laces every day," said Cody. "The stranger I saw following us had on black shoes."

"Maybe he went to a shoe store and bought black shoes," M.E. suggested.

Quinn shook his head. "I don't think so. Too expensive," Quinn said. "And where would he even buy shoes around here?"

Cody had a thought and pulled out the mysterious pen she'd found in the alcove. She opened it up and withdrew the note. "Look at this." She unrolled the small piece of paper, revealing the coded message, which was written in black ink.

"Yeah?" Quinn said. "What about it?"

"It's written with a black marker!" she said, excited.

"So?" M.E. shrugged.

"So, do you remember Matt's fingers?" Cody asked.

"Dude, there were black marks on them . . ." Luke said slowly.

" . . . which he probably got . . ." Quinn continued.

" . . . when he used a black marker . . ." M.E. added.

" . . . to color his white shoes!" Cody finished.

"Matt really has gone rogue," said Quinn. "We have to find him!"

"He has to be around here somewhere," said Cody.

"Let's try the other side of the building," Luke said, leading the group back to the front entrance. When they turned the corner, Luke pointed. "Dude, I see it!" As he ran toward the sign, Cody saw someone kneeling nearby.

It was a big kid with messy brown hair, wearing a white T-shirt and baggy jeans. A black Oakland Raiders backpack lay next to him.

Cody recognized him instantly. "Oh my gosh, it's Matt!" she called to the others and ran to catch up with Luke.

Matt the Brat was holding a black marker in his hand. He looked up to see Luke standing over him. He pushed himself up, tried to grab his backpack and missed, then started to run without it. But Luke was too fast and grabbed him by the arm. "Oh, no, you don't!" he said to Matt.

"Let go of me!" Matt jerked his arm loose.

But it was too late for him to run. The Code Busters had circled him. He was trapped.

"Matt! Where have you been?" Cody cried. "Ms. Stad is crazy-worried about you!"

"Yeah, you're in deep doo-doo, Jeffreys," Quinn said.

"You'll probably be expelled!" M.E. added.

"I don't care!" Matt said. He threw the black marker on the ground and punched his fist in the air. "I won the game! I beat all of you Code Losers and I get to meet a real Special Agent from the FBI!"

"So that's why you did all this?" Cody asked. "Just so you could win the game? What about your teammates?"

"Losers, just like you guys," he said. "I'm the best. I'm the winner!"

Matt leaned down and picked up the black marker and his backpack that still lay on the ground near the sign. As he stuffed the marker inside, Cody glanced at the sign and saw a message written in Morse code. At least, it looked like Morse code. But it was obvious to Cody that Matt had used the marker to add a bunch more dots so the message wouldn't make sense. He had made sure the Code Busters wouldn't win that visit with an FBI special agent.

Matt tried to zip up his backpack, but the zipper seemed to be stuck on something. He stuffed his hand inside and swished it around, trying to clear the opening. When he pulled his hand out, a piece of khaki-colored cloth stuck out.

"Look in his backpack!" Cody cried out.

Matt jerked his backpack to his chest in an attempt to keep it away from the others.

"Hey, what's in there, Jeffreys?" Quinn asked.

Luke yanked the backpack out of Matt's hands.

"Give me that!" Matt yelled, but Luke turned away and quickly unzipped the pack. He dumped the contents on the sidewalk. Out fell a khaki trench coat, a black baseball cap, a pair of rearview sunglasses, a fake mustache, and some folded up newspaper. Plus, there were a bunch of clues he taken from Ms. Stad.

The stranger had been Matt all along. The Code Busters stared at him in disbelief.

Matt grabbed up the items from the ground and shoved them back into his pack.

"Seriously?" Cody finally said. "*You're* the one who's been following us everywhere!"

"That's why you were always lurking nearby when we got there," Quinn said. "You knew where we'd be because you had all the clues and coordinates you stole from Ms. Stad."

"I didn't steal them!" Matt protested. "I just borrowed them."

"So your plan was to mess up the clues at each waypoint?" Quinn asked.

"It would've worked," said Matt, pouting. "I almost beat you to the first few stops. And I got here first!"

"You scared us half to death," M.E. said, scowling at Matt. "We thought you were some kind of spy who was stalking us!"

Luke shook his head. "I wasn't really scared."

"Me, either," Quinn added. "We figured it was you all along."

Cody knew they were trying to act like they hadn't been fooled. "Well, we *were* a little weirded out by you. Not cool."

Matt shrugged. "Admit it. I'm a better spy than all of you put together. I made up my own secret codes. And I'm going to join the FBI someday and be a real Code Buster."

Cody frowned and shook her head. Mika was right about why Matt the Brat had done all of this— spied on them, tried to ruin the game. He hadn't just wanted to win the prize.

Matt the Brat really wanted to be a Code Buster.

* * * * *

Cody texted Ms. Stad and Mr. Littlefield to let them know where they were—and that they had finally found Matt. Since the Spy Museum was only two blocks away from the FBI building, Ms. Stad and Mr. Littlefield arrived there minutes later, relieved to see the missing boy and the Code Busters safe and sound.

Matt started to explain to her why he had gone off on his own, but Ms. Stad made it clear he was in big trouble. Furthermore, he would not win the prize because he had broken the rules. While the Code Busters told the teacher and chaperone what had happened as they walked back to the Spy Museum, Matt pouted every step of the way.

"Why didn't you answer our texts?" Cody asked Mr. Littlefield.

"What are texts?" the chaperone answered.

The kids giggled. Mr. Littlefield was a computer engineer who knew LEET code but didn't know what a text was? "Never mind," Cody said.

When they arrived, Ms. Stad escorted Matt onto

the bus, and had Mr. Littlefield sit next to him to make sure nothing else happened.

"Well, you didn't follow my orders to wait until the chaperone came, but I understand why you did what you did, and I'm grateful you found Matt," Ms. Stad said, giving each one a hug as they stood by the bus. "I just wish you'd told me in case you got into trouble. But thank you for saving the trip for the rest of the students—except for Matt, of course. Tomorrow morning he'll be flying back home with Mr. Littlefield."

Cody couldn't help feeling sorry for Matt the Brat. He was always doing something to get himself in trouble. What he had done—going off on his own—could have been really dangerous, so he deserved to be in trouble. Still, it was too bad that he would miss the rest of the trip. Cody had a thought.

"Ms. Stad," Cody said to her teacher.

"Yes, Cody," Ms. Stad replied.

"I was thinking. Maybe instead of sending Matt home, he could just miss one of the other sites. That way he'd still get to learn about history and stuff, but also learn a lesson about leaving the group. Maybe you could have him help you prepare for the next hunt. He's a really good artist. I've seen some of his drawings. He could draw some of the codes."

Ms. Stad frown turned to a soft smile. "Not a bad idea, Cody. He'll learn a lot more by staying than he will be being sent home. I'm sure I can come up with some things for him to do to help me while you all are at the Cherry Blossom Festival."

Cody smiled back at her teacher. Ms. Stad was firm, but she was also fair. And maybe Matt really would learn something this time.

"How's Mrs. Takeda?" M.E. asked.

"She'll be fine," Ms. Stad said. "I talked to Mika and she said her mother has a cast on her ankle, but they'll both be joining us on the rest of our site-seeing tour. Mrs. Takeda will use crutches to get around. She's a trooper."

"Are they still at the hospital?" Cody asked. She was eager to see her new friend Mika and tell her what had happened.

At that moment, a taxicab pulled up in front of the Spy Museum. The back door opened and a girl with short dark hair stepped out, along with another one of the chaperones. As soon as the girl turned to face the group, the Code Busters burst out with laughter.

Mika was wearing a fake mustache!

"Mika!" they all said, rushing up to meet her while Ms. Stad paid the cab fare.

"You're back!" Cody said. "We missed you!"

Mika smiled. "Just for a few minutes. The doctor is still taking care of my mom, but I wanted to come back and thank you for your help," she said.

"We're glad she's going to be all right," M.E. said.

"Guess what?" Quinn said. "We found Matt!"

"That's great!" Mika said.

"That's not all," Ms. Stad said, returning to the group as the cab drove away. "They also won the Spy Hunt." She turned to the Code Busters. "You found all the clues, solved all the puzzles, and made it all the way to the end—without cheating. I think you've brought a whole new meaning to the word CODE in Code Busters. Clever—you were smart. Optimistic—you never gave up. Daring—you were brave. And Enterprising—you were creative in the way that you solved the puzzles and found Matt. I'm very proud of you. You deserve to have the special meeting with my nephew, the FBI agent."

"Sweet!" Luke said.

"Awesome!" Quinn agreed.

M.E. just squealed in excitement and clapped her hands.

Cody turned to the others and finger-spelled a question:

*Code Busters' Key and Solution found on pp. 151, 157.*

They all gave Cody a thumbs up—the universal code for agreement. Cody smiled at the new girl. "Mika, how would you like to join the Code Busters Club? You're really good at cracking codes and you'd make a great member."

The others nodded and smiled warmly.

Tears formed in Mika's eyes. "I'd like that," she said softly. "This is the best birthday ever."

"Today's your birthday?" Cody said, surprised

Mika had kept it a secret.

Mika nodded shyly.

"Wow. How do you say Happy Birthday in Japanese?" Quinn asked.

"*Tanjoubi omedetou*," Mika said.

"*Tanjoubi omedetou!*" the four Code Busters said together. They gave the birthday girl a group hug.

"*Arigato gozaimasu!*" Mika said, grinning. "I'm so glad to be a member of the Code Busters Club!"

Cody was glad too. She wondered what new adventures—and codes—awaited them when they returned home. Although their next field trip wasn't for several weeks, she was looking forward to the ferry ride to Angel Island, called the "Ellis Island of the West." Ms. Stad had told them there were coded messages carved into the walls of the abandoned immigration station, left by people seeking a new life in America, just like Mika. She'd even given them a Japanese haiku to study on their flight home.

*Ferry to the shore,*
*Scavenge for some hidden finds,*
*Snap, but do not take . . .*

# CODE BUSTERS'

# Key Book
# &
# Solutions

## Japanese Kanji Numbers:

| 〇 | 一 | 二 | 三 | 四 | 五 | 六 | 七 | 八 | 九 |
|---|---|---|---|---|---|---|---|---|---|
| 0 | 1 | 2 | 3 | 4 | 5 | 6 | 7 | 8 | 9 |

## George Washington's Code:

| a | b | c | d | e | f | g | h | i | j | k | l | m |
|---|---|---|---|---|---|---|---|---|---|---|---|---|
| — | | | + | # | ? | | □ | ⊡ | ; | ⊏ | ⊡ | ⊐ |

| n | o | p | q | r | s | t | u | v | w | x | y | z |
|---|---|---|---|---|---|---|---|---|---|---|---|---|
| | L | = | ∏ | ∏ | ○ | ⊙ | ㄱ | ㄱ | ∧ | ∨ | < | > |

## Alphanumeric Code:

| 1 | 2 | 3 | 4 | 5 | 6 | 7 | 8 | 9 | 10 | 11 | 12 | 13 | 14 | 15 |
|---|---|---|---|---|---|---|---|---|---|---|---|---|---|---|
| A | B | C | D | E | F | G | H | I | J | K | L | M | N | O |

| 16 | 17 | 18 | 19 | 20 | 21 | 22 | 23 | 24 | 25 | 26 |
|---|---|---|---|---|---|---|---|---|---|---|
| P | Q | R | S | T | U | V | W | X | Y | Z |

# International Morse Code:

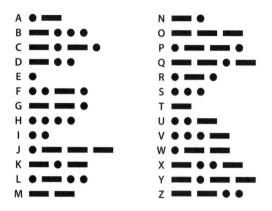

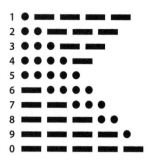

| | | | | |
|---|---|---|---|---|
| A | • ▬ | N | ▬ • | 1 • ▬ ▬ ▬ ▬ |
| B | ▬ • • • | O | ▬ ▬ ▬ | 2 • • ▬ ▬ ▬ |
| C | ▬ • ▬ • | P | • ▬ ▬ • | 3 • • • ▬ ▬ |
| D | ▬ • • | Q | ▬ ▬ • ▬ | 4 • • • • ▬ |
| E | • | R | • ▬ • | 5 • • • • • |
| F | • • ▬ • | S | • • • | 6 ▬ • • • • |
| G | ▬ ▬ • | T | ▬ | 7 ▬ ▬ • • • |
| H | • • • • | U | • • ▬ | 8 ▬ ▬ ▬ • • |
| I | • • | V | • • • ▬ | 9 ▬ ▬ ▬ ▬ • |
| J | • ▬ ▬ ▬ | W | • ▬ ▬ | 0 ▬ ▬ ▬ ▬ ▬ |
| K | ▬ • ▬ | X | ▬ • • ▬ | |
| L | • ▬ • • | Y | ▬ • ▬ ▬ | |
| M | ▬ ▬ | Z | ▬ ▬ • • | |

# Pigpen Code:
Key Version 1

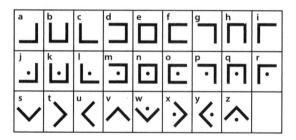

Key Version 2

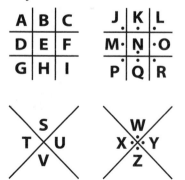

## Finger Spelling:

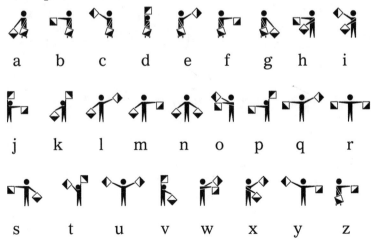

a  b  c  d  e  f  g  h

i  j  k  l  m  n  o  p  q  r

s  t  u  v  w  x  y  z

1  2  3  4  5  6  7  8  9

## Semaphore Code:

a  b  c  d  e  f  g  h  i

j  k  l  m  n  o  p  q  r

s  t  u  v  w  x  y  z

## LEET Code:

| | | | |
|---|---|---|---|
| A = 4 | H = # | O = ( ) | V = \/ |
| B = 8 | I = ! | P = \|* | W = \/\/ |
| C = ( | J = _\| | Q = (,) | X = * |
| D = \|) | K = \|< | R = \|2 | Y = \\|/ |
| E = 3 | L = \|_ | S = $ | Z = 2 |
| F = \|= | M = /\/\ | T = + | |
| G = 6 | N = /\/ | U = (_) | |

## Phonetic Alphabet:

| | | |
|---|---|---|
| A = Alpha | J = Juliet | S = Sierra |
| B = Bravo | K = Kilo | T = Tango |
| C = Charlie | L = Lima | U = Uniform |
| D = Delta | M = Mike | V = Victor |
| E = Echo | N = November | W = Whisker |
| F = Foxtrot | O = Oscar | X = X-ray |
| G = Golf | P = Papa | Y = Yankee |
| H = Hotel | Q = Quebec | Z = Zulu |
| I = India | R = Romeo | |

Chapter 1 Solutions

*Pig Latin:* **Is it time for recess?**

*Acronyms:*

*APB:* **all-points bulletin**

*AWOL:* **absent without official leave**

*BLT:* **bacon, lettuce and tomato**

*BOLO:* **be on the lookout**

*BRB:* **be right back**

*DIY:* **do it yourself**

*EMT:* **emergency medical technician**

*FAQ:* **frequently asked questions**

*FYI:* **for your information**

*LOL:* **laugh out loud**

*OMW:* **on my way**

*PBJ:* **peanut butter and jelly**

*P.I.:* **private investigator**

*S&R:* **search and rescue**

*UFO:* **unidentified flying object**

*Cartoon Drawings:*

**Eye (I) Watch Ewe (You) Mat (Matt)**

## Chapter 2 Solutions

*Washington Code:*

**What is your code name?**

**EMME (M.E.)**

**Kuel Dude**

**Lock & Key**

**Code Red**

**I want a decoder ring**

**Spies are cool**

**Can you read this?**

**Let's wear disguises**

*Japanese numbers:*

**23 – 8 – 15**

**23 – 1 – 14 – 20 – 19**

**20 – 15**

**7 – 15**

**15 – 14**

**1**

**19 – 16 – 25**

**8 – 21 – 14 – 20**

*Japanese number code message:* **Who wants to go on a spy hunt?**

## Chapter 3 Solutions

*Washington Code:*

**Create a legend (background) for your cover (secret identity).**

**I spy you.**

## Chapter 4 Solutions

*Morse Code:*

**Welcome to the Spy Museum!**

**SOS**

## Chapter 5 Solutions

*Washington Monument coordinates:*

**38° 53' 22.08377" N   77° 2' 6.86378" W**

*Acrostic code:* **FATHER OF OUR COUNTRY**

## Chapter 6 Solutions

*Pigpen:* **The castle has trap doors, hidden tunnels, and secret rooms.**

*Morse Code:* **Don't look now, but I think we're being followed.**

## Chapter 7 Solution

*Confederate Code:* **House divided cannot stand**

## Chapter 8 Solutions

*Cartoon Message:* **Matt the Master Spy Was Here**

*Semaphore:* **Let's go find Matt**

## Chapter 9 Solutions

*Phonetic Alphabet Code:* **Stad coming this way**

*Phonetic Alphabet Code:* **Think fast!**

*Finger Spelling:* **Matt**

*LEET Code:* **Allosaurus medius, Ceratosaurus nasicornis, Stegosaurus stenops, Triceratops alticornis**

*Phonetic Alphabet Code:* **Here you'll find: Moon Rock, Lunar Module, Spirit of St. Louis, Pioneer Space Probe, and Mercury Friendship Spacecraft.**

## Chapter 10 Solution

*LEET Code:* **Sorry, we had to leave. Will explain later.**

## Chapter 11 Solutions

*LEET Code:* **At the air and space museum, one more waypoint to go, then we will be back.**

*Washington Code:* **Fidelity, bravery, integrity**

## Chapter 12 Solutions

*Finger Spelling:* **Can Mika join the Code Busters Club?**

## Chapter Title Translations (Finger Spelling):

*Chapter 1:* **DIY Codes in the Classroom**

*Chapter 2:* **Washington Code FYI**

*Chapter 3:* **A Spy or UFO at the Door**

*Chapter 4:* **OMW to the Spy Museum**

*Chapter 5:* **An APB for Mika**

*Chapter 6:* **Race to the Waypoint ASAP**

*Chapter 7:* **BOLO for a Spy**

*Chapter 8:* **Matt the Brat is MIA**

*Chapter 9:* **AWOL Student**

*Chapter 10:* **Call the EMT**

*Chapter 11:* **SOS—Stop Our Stalker**

*Chapter 12:* **A New Code Buster**

*For more adventures with the Code Busters Club, go to www.CodeBustersClub.com.*

There you'll find:

1. Full dossiers for Cody, Quinn, Luke, and M.E.
2. Their blogs
3. More codes
4. More coded messages to solve
5. Clues to the next book
6. A map of the Code Busters neighborhood, school, and mystery
7. A contest to win your name in the next Code Busters book.

# Suggestions for How Teachers Can Use the Code Busters Club Series in the Classroom

Kids love codes. They will want to "solve" the codes in this novel before looking up the solutions. This means they will be practicing skills that are necessary to their class work in several courses, but in a non-pressured way.

The codes in this book vary in level of difficulty so there is something for students of every ability. The codes move from a simple code wheel—Caesar's Cipher wheel—to more widely accepted "code" languages such as Morse code, semaphore and Braille.

In a mathematics classroom, the codes in this book can easily be used as motivational devices to teach problem-solving and reasoning skills. Both of these have become important elements in the curriculum at all grade levels. The emphasis throughout the book on regarding codes as patterns gives students a great deal of practice in one of the primary strategies of problem solving. The strategy of "Looking for a Pattern" is basic to much of mathematics. The resolving of codes demonstrates how important patterns are. These codes can lead to discussions of the logic behind why they "work," (problem solving). The teacher can then have the students create their own codes (problem formulation) and try sending secret messages to one another, while other students try to "break the code." Developing and resolving these new codes will require a great deal of careful reasoning on the part of the students. The class might also wish to do some practical research in statistics, to determine which letters occur most  frequently in the English language. (E, T, A, O, and N are the first five most widely used letters and should appear most often in coded messages.)

This book may also be used in other classroom areas of study such as social studies, with its references to code-breaking machines, American Sign Language, and Braille. This book raises questions such as, "Why would semaphore be important today? Where is it still used?"

In the English classroom, spelling is approached as a "deciphering code." The teacher may also suggest the students do some outside reading. They might read a biography of Samuel Morse or Louis Braille, or even the Sherlock Holmes mystery "The Adventure of the Dancing Men."

This book also refers to modern texting on cell phones and computers as a form of code. Students could explain what the various "code" abbreviations they use mean today and why they are used.                    —Dr. Stephen Krulik

*Dr. Stephen Krulik has a distinguished career as a professor of mathematics education. Professor emeritus at Temple University, he received the 2011 Lifetime Achievement Award from the National Council of Teachers of Mathematics.*